W9-BJB-804

NARWHAL'S

MONODON MONOCEROS

SCHOOL OF AWESOMENESS

BEN CLANTON

tundra

IN MEMORY OF THE KIND, CURIOUS AND CREATIVE CROSLEY JAYNE BUCHNER

AND WITH MY THANKS TO PROF. AMADOU FOFANA, SUE BROWN, GLENDA SKEIM, PROF. JEANNE CLARK, PROF. JOYCE MILLEN, PROF. REBECCA DOBKINS, MIKE MCGARVEY, ALLEN SLATER, CINDY GALVIN AND ALL THE EDUCATORS WHO HAVE CHALLENGED AND INSPIRED ME. ALSO TO TEACHERS WHO HAVE HELPED MY BOOKS FIND READERS, ESPECIALLY MICHELE O'HARE!

Text and illustrations copyright © 2021 by Ben Clanton
This paperback edition published by Tundra Books, 2023

Tundra Books, an imprint of Tundra Book Group,
a division of Penguin Random House of Canada Limited

All rights reserved. The use of any part of this publication reproduced, transmitted in any form or by any means, electronic, mechanical, photocopying, recording, or otherwise, or stored in a retrieval system, without the prior written consent of the publisher — or, in case of photocopying or other reprographic copying, a licence from the Canadian Copyright Licensing Agency — is an infringement of the copyright law.

Library and Archives Canada Cataloguing in Publication

Title: Narwhal's school of awesomeness / Ben Clanton.
Names: Clanton, Ben, 1988- author, illustrator.
Series: Clanton, Ben, 1988- Narwhal and Jelly book ; 6.
Description: Series statement: A Narwhal and Jelly book ; 6
Identifiers: Canadiana 20220171513 | ISBN 9780735262553 (softcover)
Subjects: LCGFT: Comics (Graphic works) | LCGFT: Graphic novels.
Classification: LCC PZ7.7.C53 Nar 2023 | DDC j741.5/973—dc23

Published simultaneously in the United States of America by Tundra Books of Northern New York, an imprint of Tundra Book Group, a division of Penguin Random House of Canada Limited

Library of Congress Control Number: 2020952297

Edited by Tara Walker and Peter Phillips
Designed by Ben Clanton | Coloring by Jaime Temairik and Ben Clanton
The artwork in this book was rendered in colored pencil, watercolor and ink, and colored digitally.
The text was set in a typeface based on hand-lettering by Ben Clanton.

Photos: (chalkboard) © STUDIO DREAM/Shutterstock; (strawberry) © Valentina Razumova/Shutterstock; (waffle) © Tiger Images/Shutterstock; (pineapple) © daysupa/Shutterstock; (fries) © Drozhzhina Elena/Shutterstock; (scales) © Natalia Kudryavtseva/Shutterstock; (scales 2) © HPL17/Shutterstock

Printed in China

www.penguinrandomhouse.ca

2   3   4   5   27   26   25   24   23

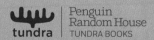

tundra | Penguin Random House TUNDRA BOOKS

CONTENTS

5 GO FISH!

33 A GREAT GROUP OF
FUN FACTS

35 WAFFLEMATICS

43 SCIENCE SQUAD VS.
FUN FINDERS

57 TAG! YOU'RE ~~X~~ AWESOME!

65 SUPER WAFFLE AND
STRAWBERRY SIDEKICK VS.
THE MUCUS MONSTER

71 W+

GO FISH!

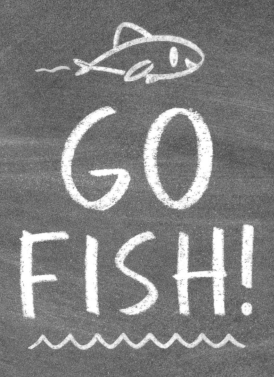

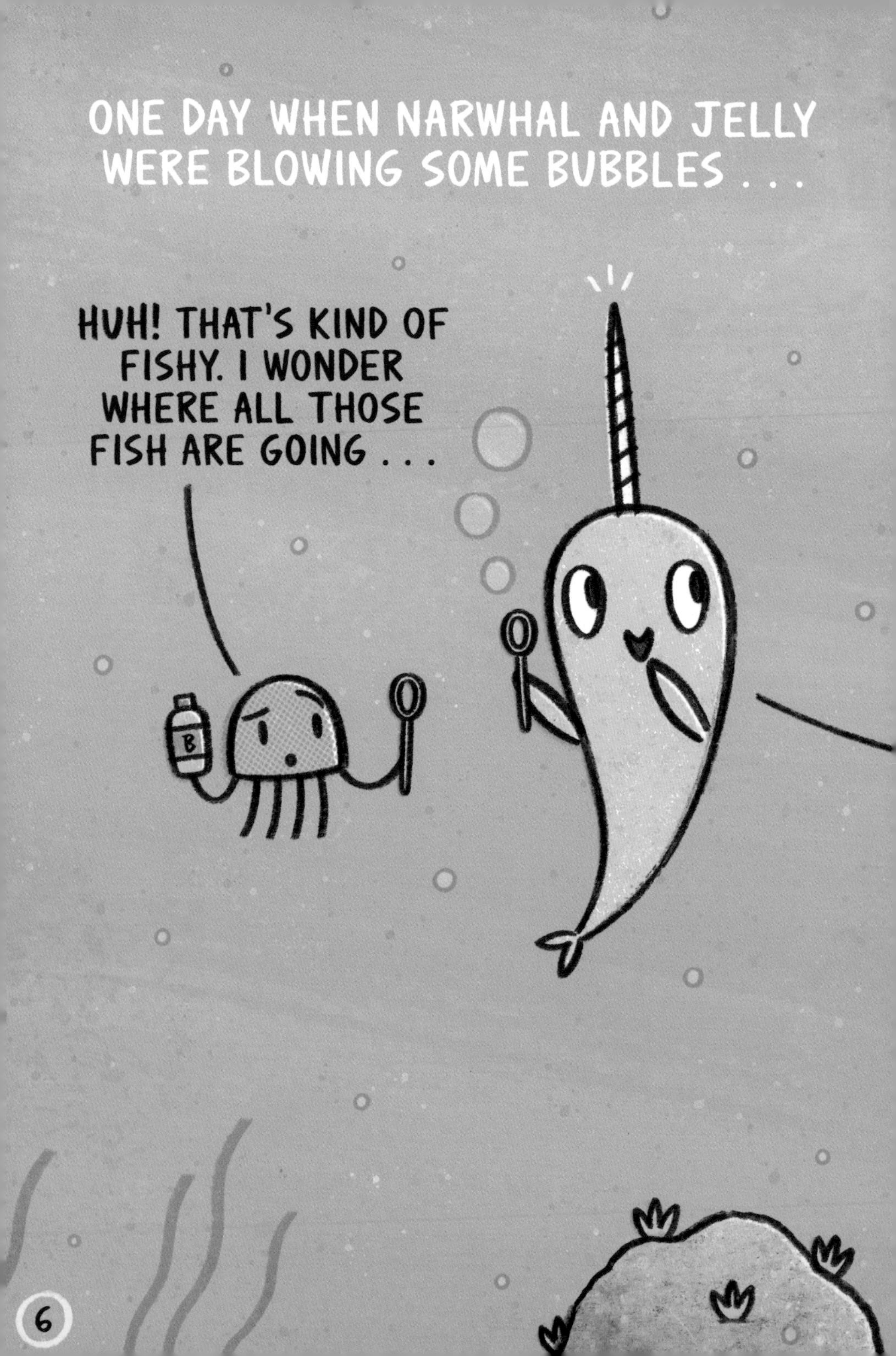
ONE DAY WHEN NARWHAL AND JELLY WERE BLOWING SOME BUBBLES . . .
HUH! THAT'S KIND OF FISHY. I WONDER WHERE ALL THOSE FISH ARE GOING . . .
B

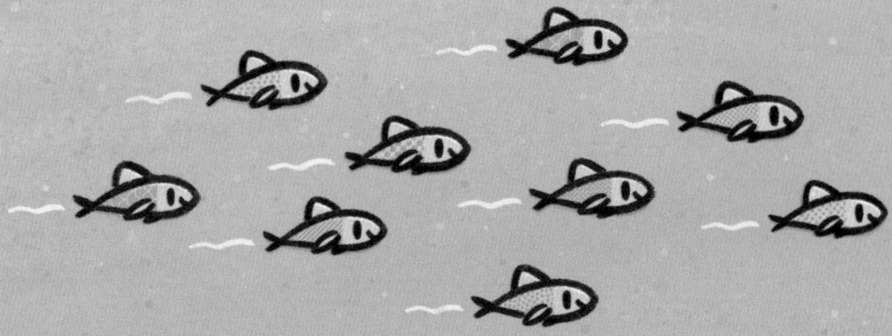

HMMM!
MAYBE THEY'RE . . .

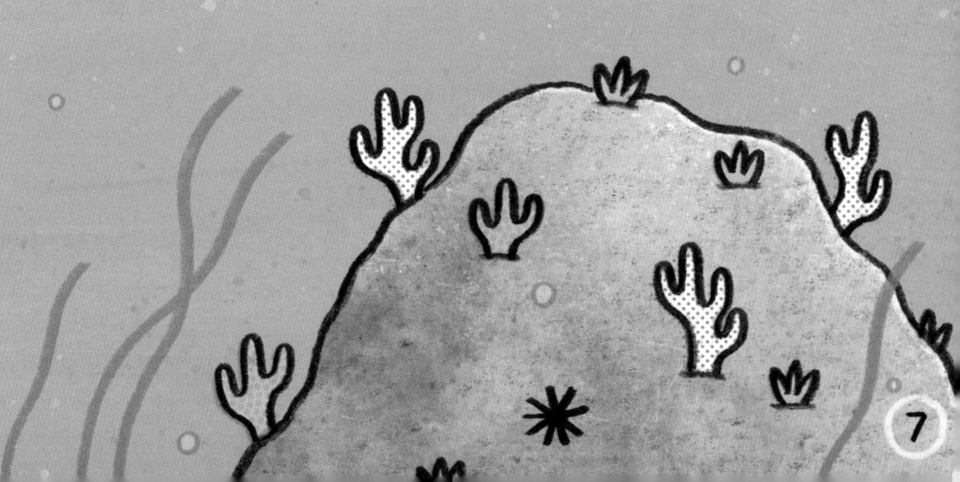

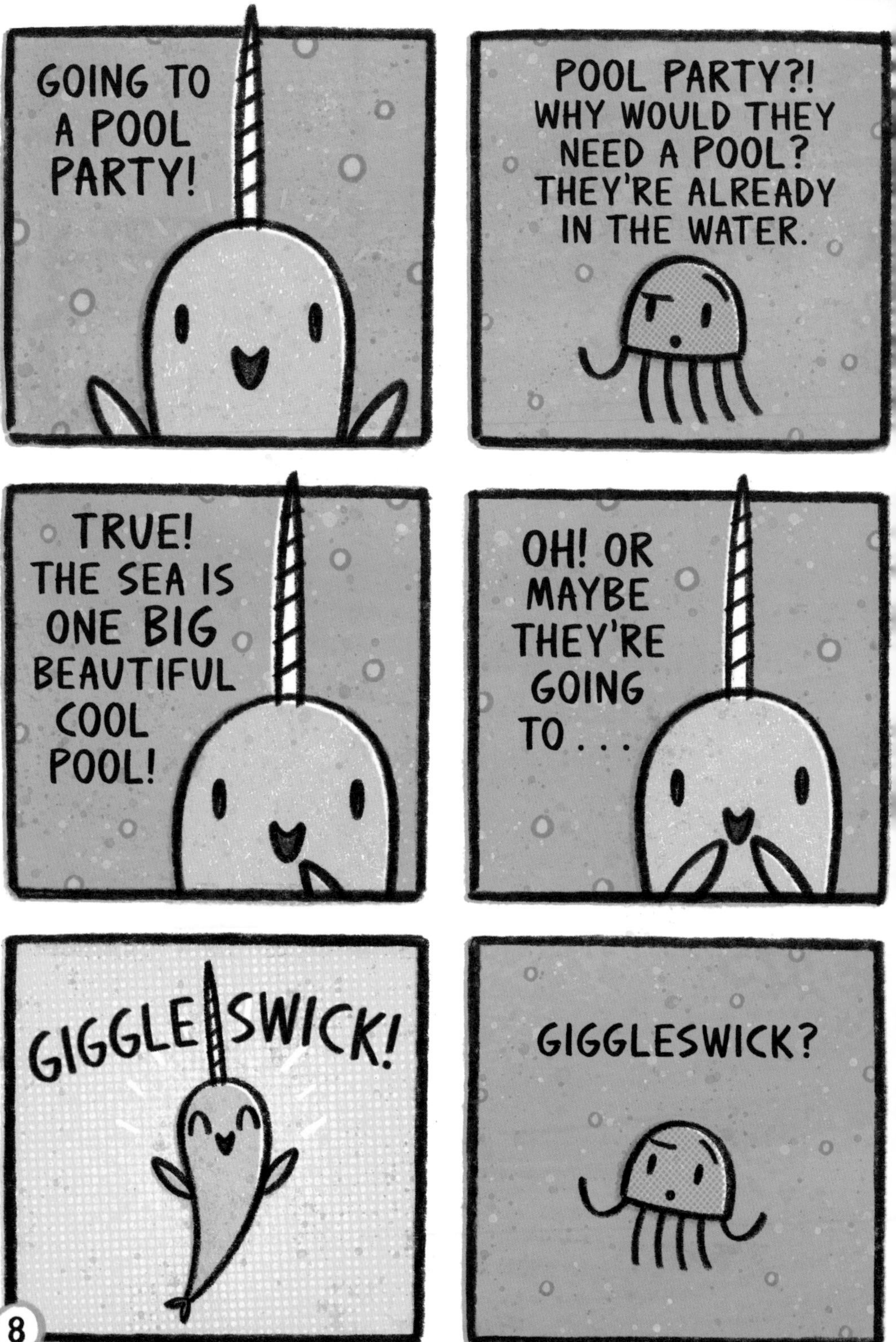
GOING TO A POOL PARTY!
POOL PARTY?! WHY WOULD THEY NEED A POOL? THEY'RE ALREADY IN THE WATER.
TRUE! THE SEA IS ONE BIG BEAUTIFUL COOL POOL!
OH! OR MAYBE THEY'RE GOING TO . . .
GIGGLESWICK!
GIGGLESWICK?

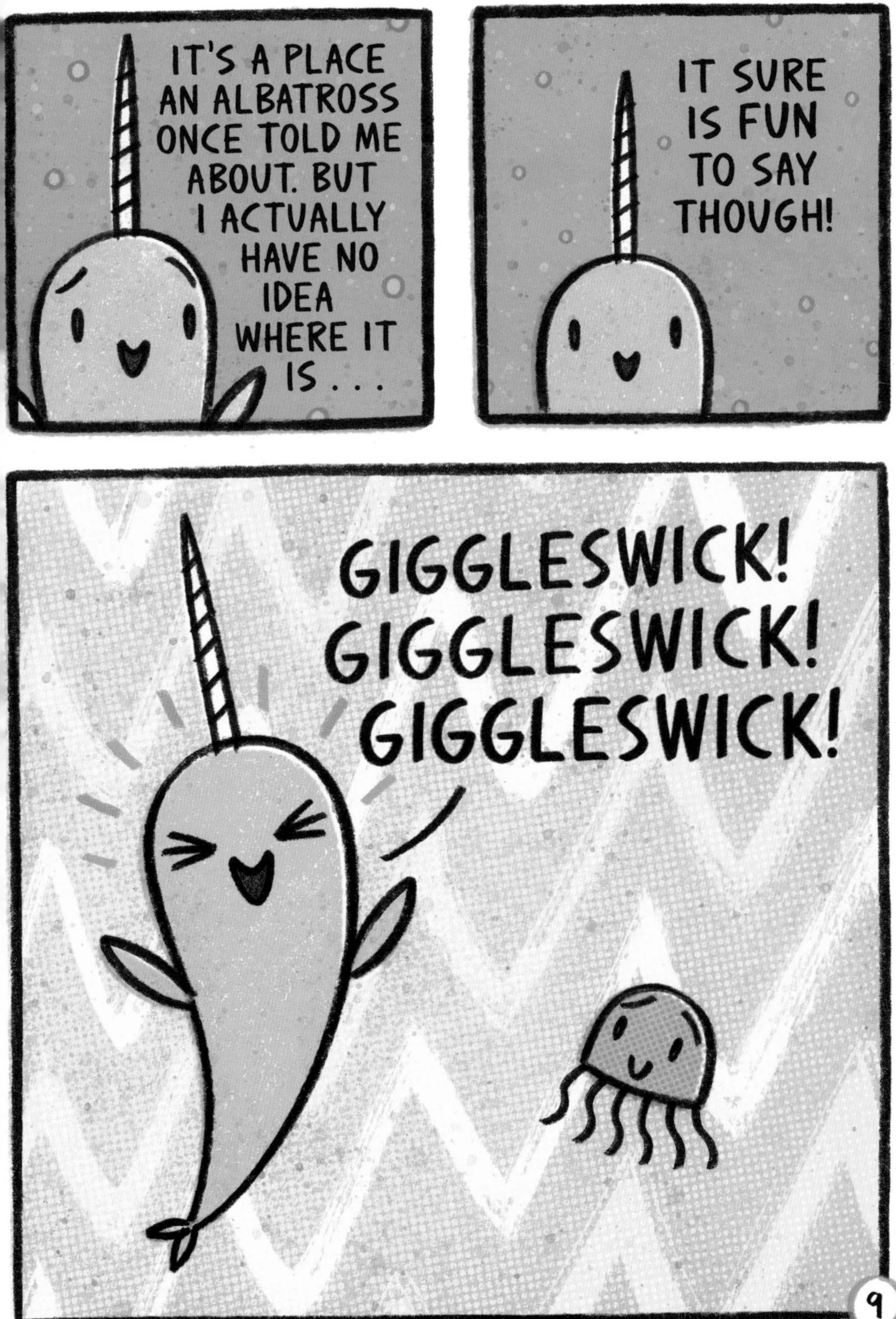
IT'S A PLACE AN ALBATROSS ONCE TOLD ME ABOUT. BUT I ACTUALLY HAVE NO IDEA WHERE IT IS . . .
IT SURE IS FUN TO SAY THOUGH!
GIGGLESWICK! GIGGLESWICK! GIGGLESWICK!

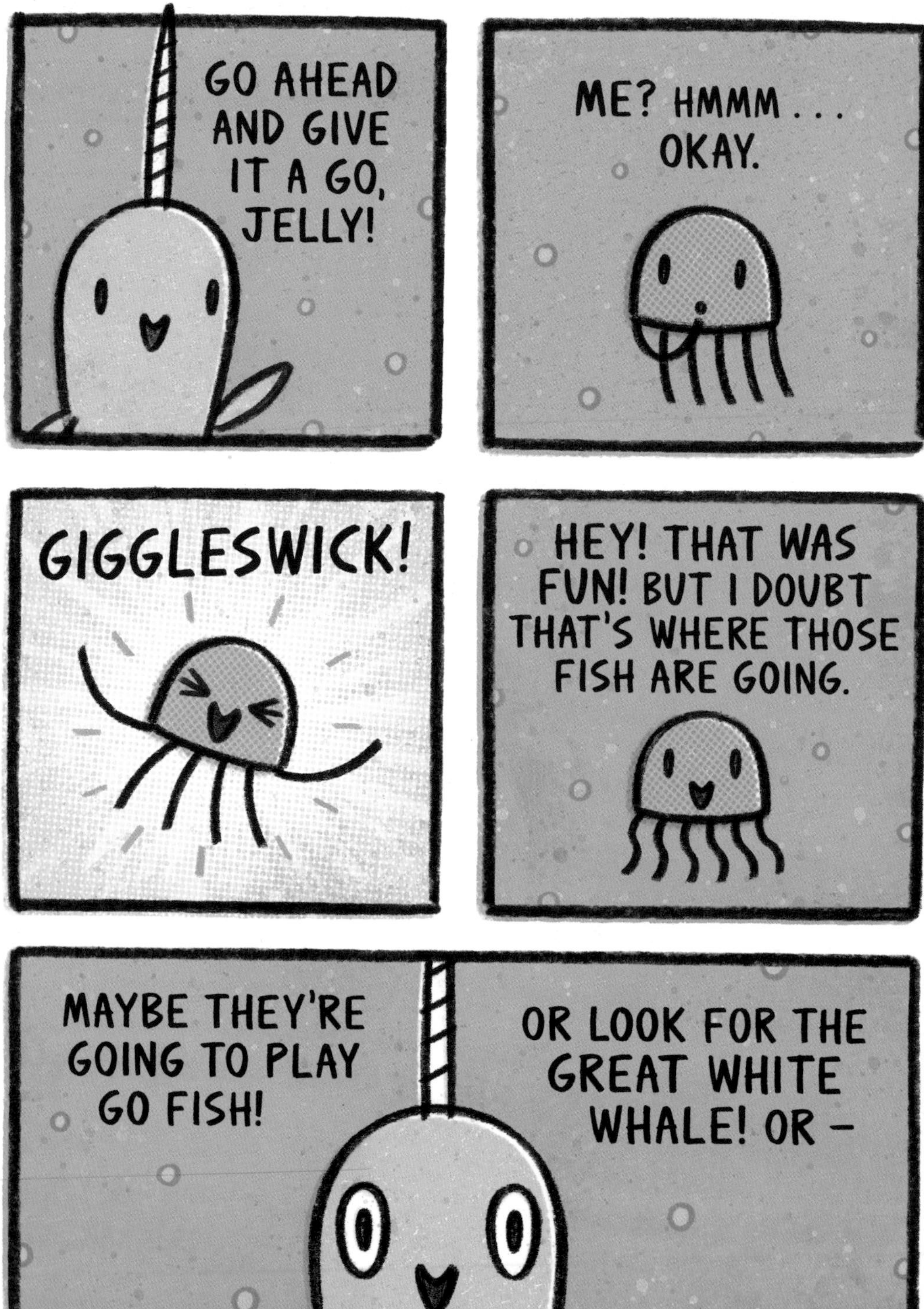
GO AHEAD AND GIVE IT A GO, JELLY!
ME? HMMM . . . OKAY.
GIGGLESWICK!
HEY! THAT WAS FUN! BUT I DOUBT THAT'S WHERE THOSE FISH ARE GOING.
MAYBE THEY'RE GOING TO PLAY GO FISH!
OR LOOK FOR THE GREAT WHITE WHALE! OR –

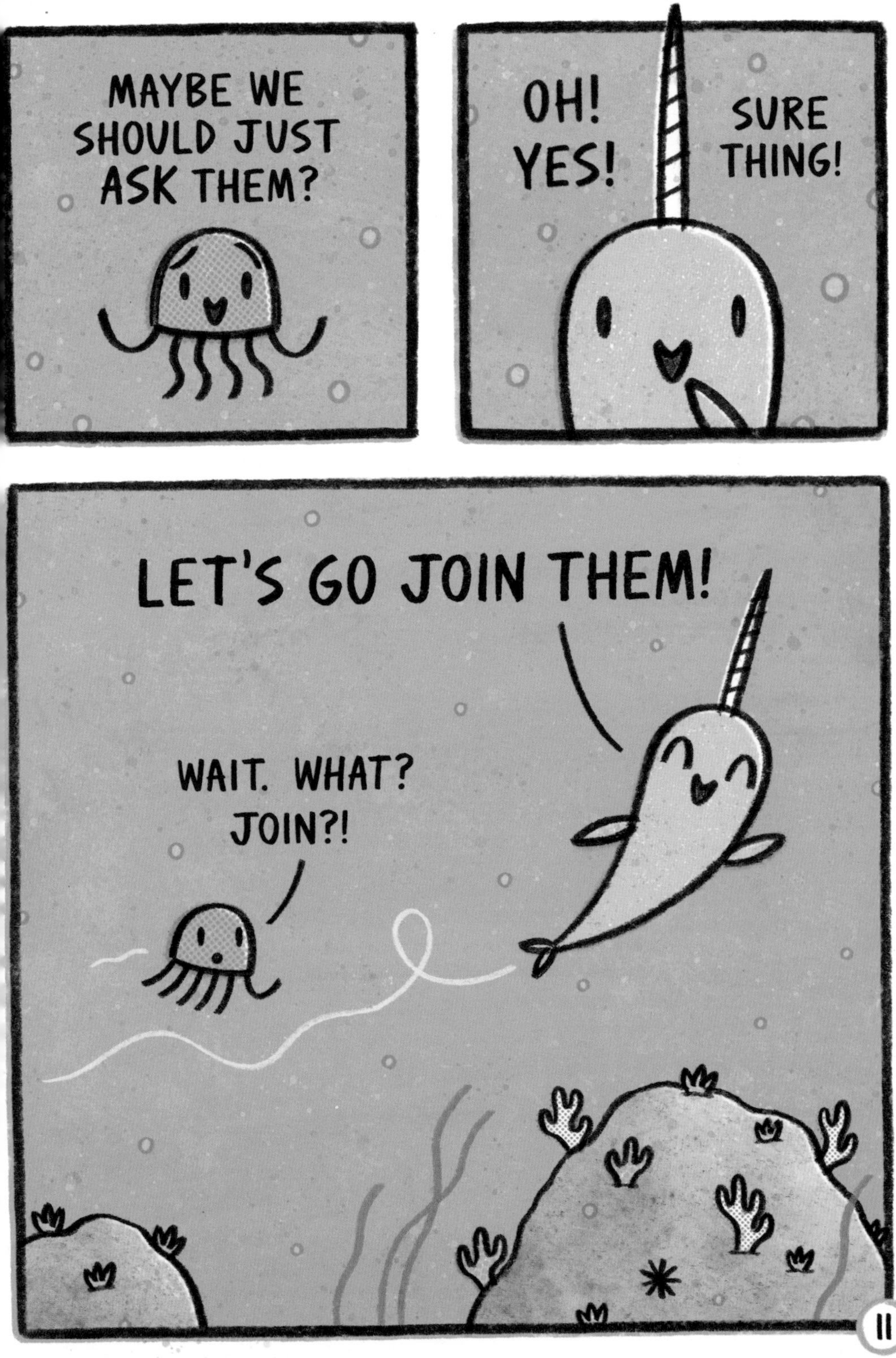
MAYBE WE SHOULD JUST ASK THEM?
OH! YES!
SURE THING!
LET'S GO JOIN THEM!
WAIT. WHAT? JOIN?!

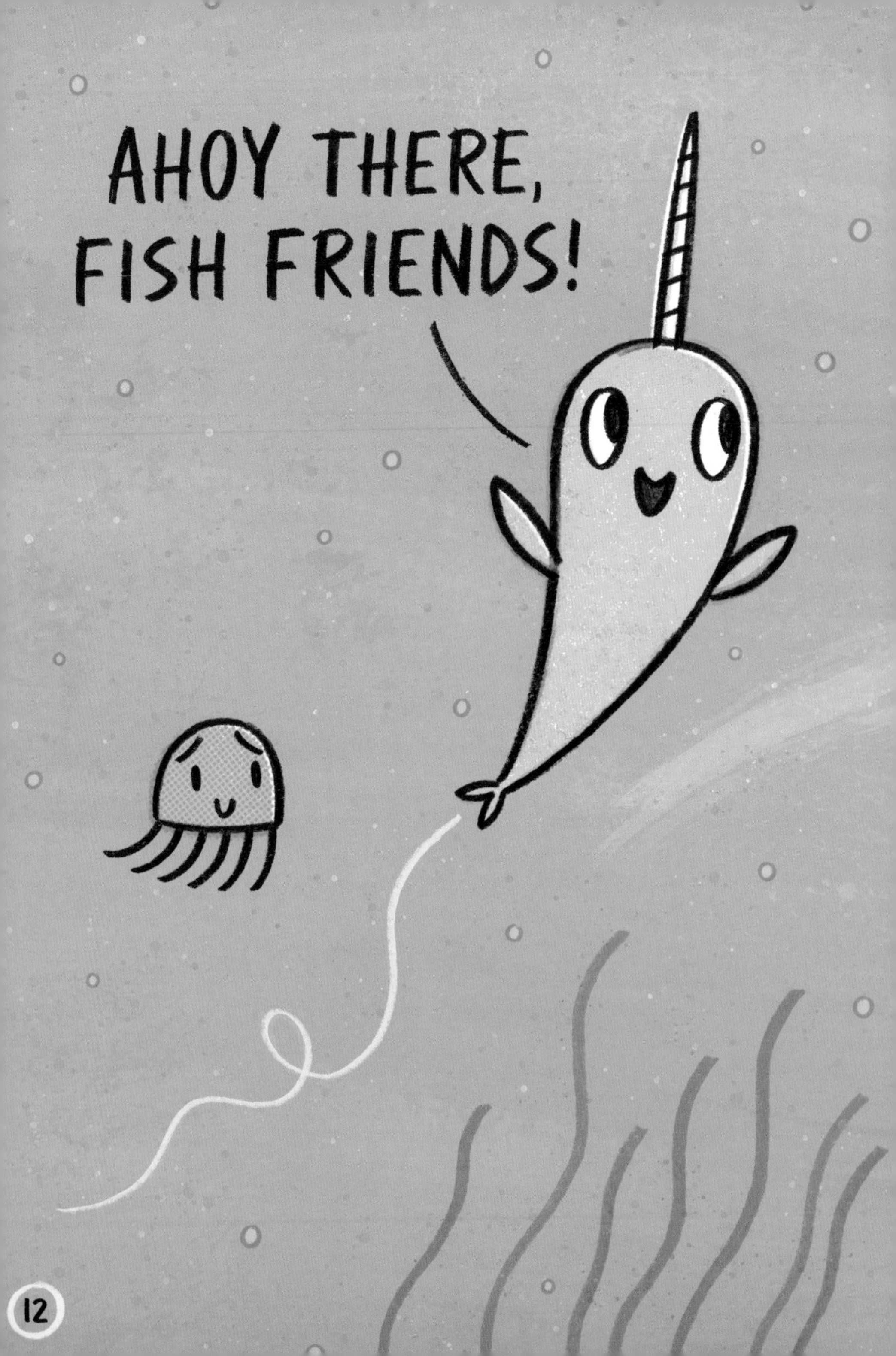
AHOY THERE, FISH FRIENDS!

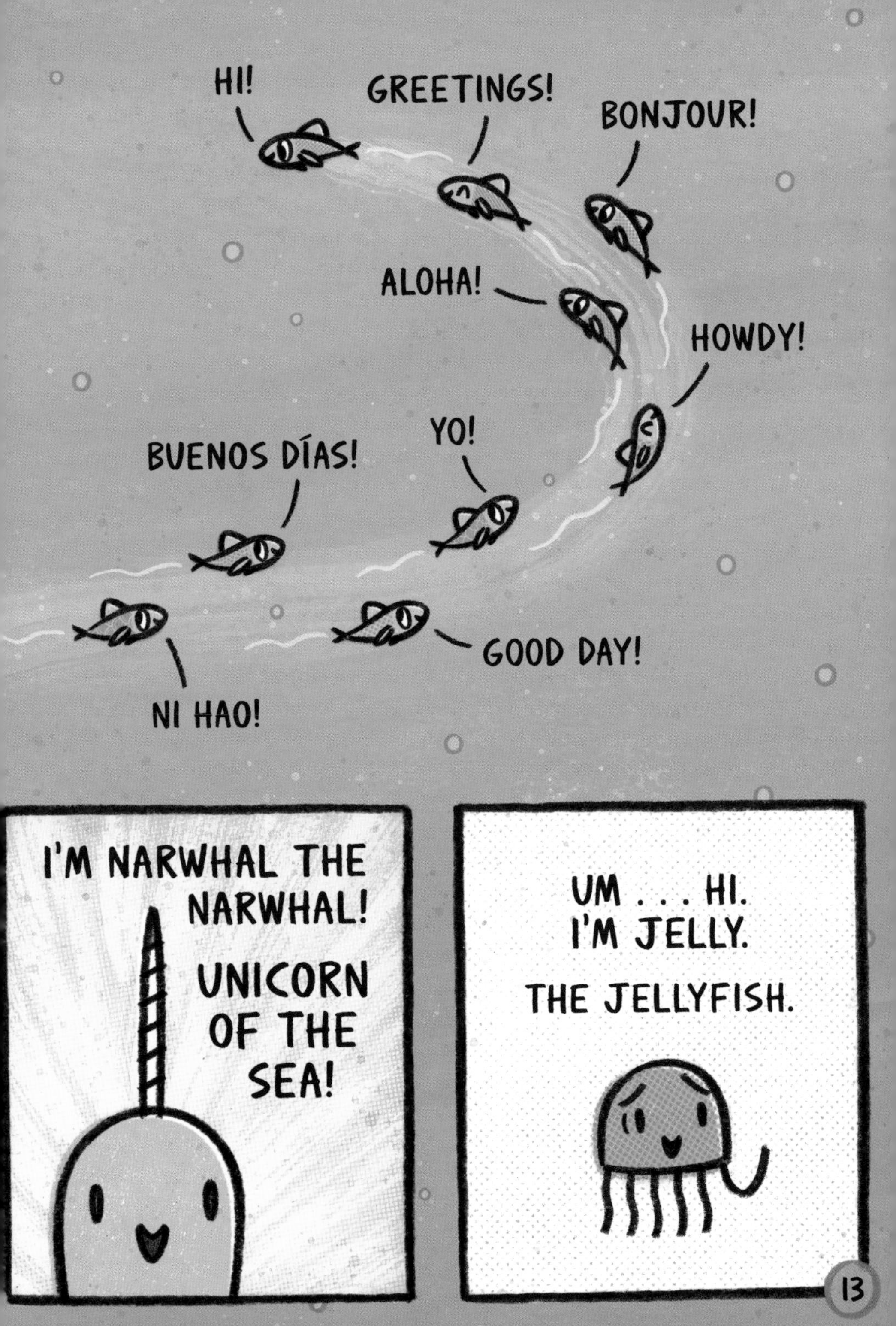
HI!
GREETINGS!
BONJOUR!
ALOHA!
HOWDY!
YO!
BUENOS DÍAS!
GOOD DAY!
NI HAO!
I'M NARWHAL THE NARWHAL!
UNICORN OF THE SEA!
UM . . . HI. I'M JELLY.
THE JELLYFISH.

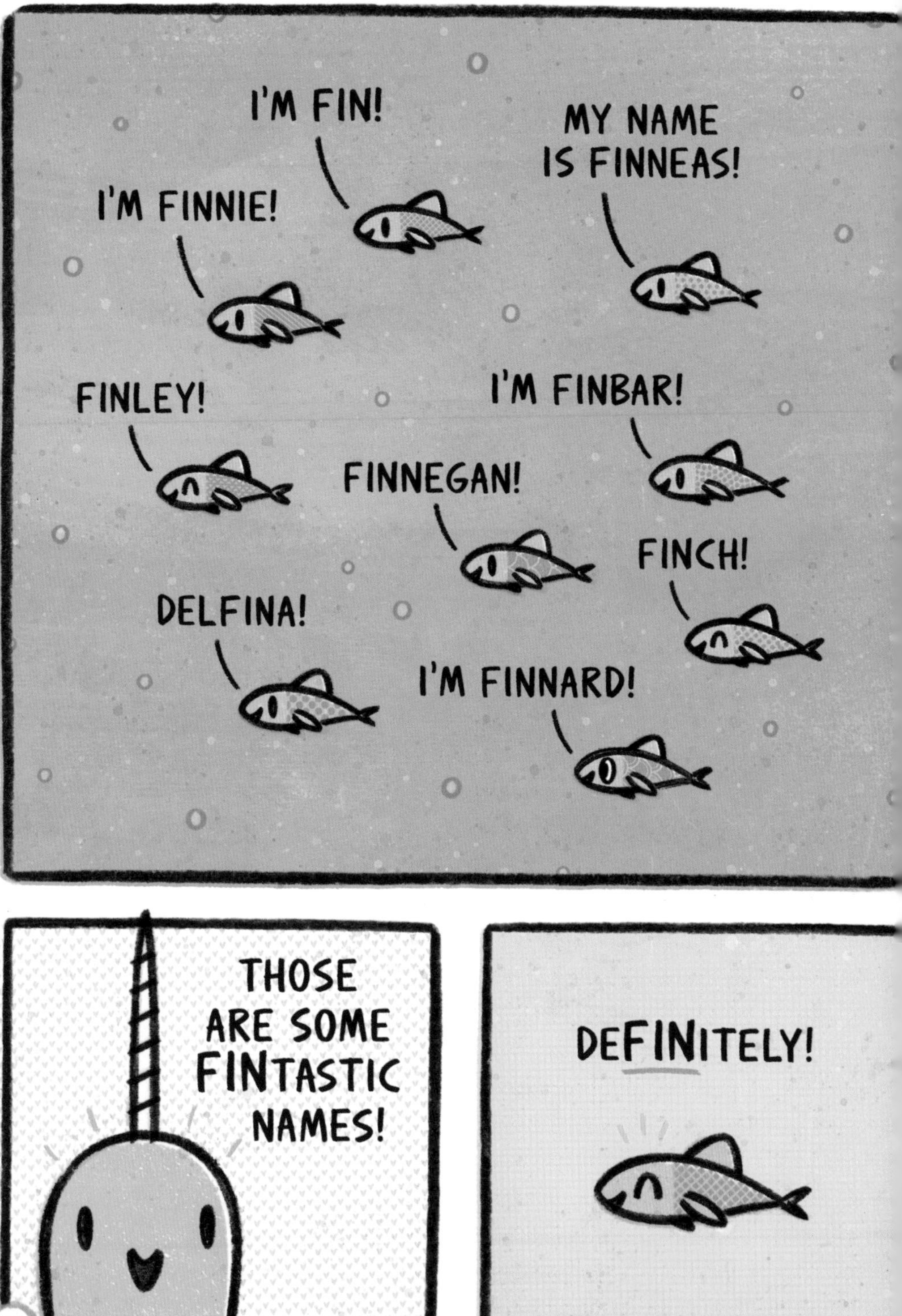
I'M FIN!
MY NAME IS FINNEAS!
I'M FINNIE!
FINLEY!
I'M FINBAR!
FINNEGAN!
FINCH!
DELFINA!
I'M FINNARD!
THOSE ARE SOME FINTASTIC NAMES!
DEFINITELY!

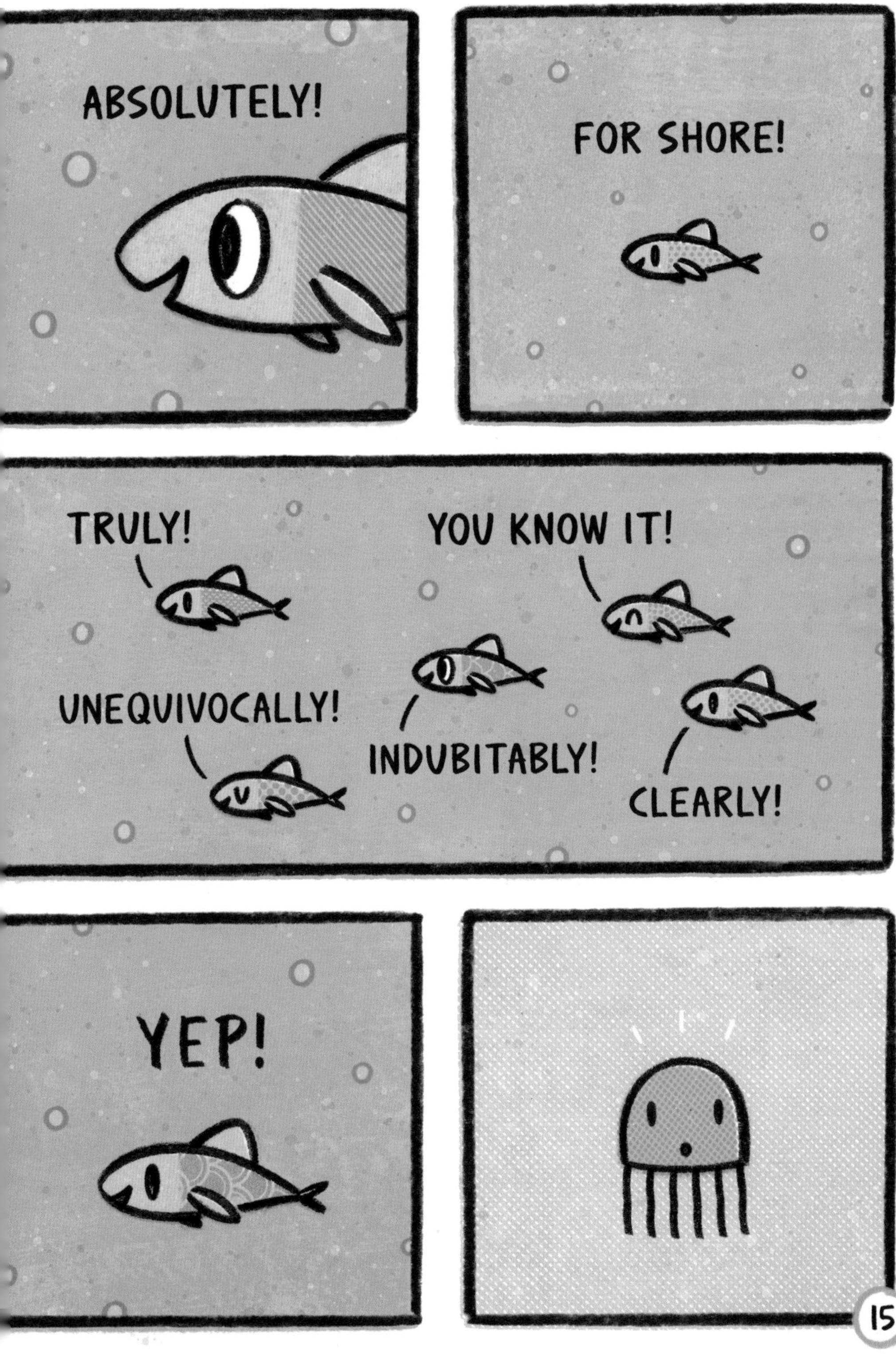
ABSOLUTELY!
FOR SHORE!
TRULY!
YOU KNOW IT!
UNEQUIVOCALLY!
INDUBITABLY!
CLEARLY!
YEP!

WHERE ARE YOU ALL GOING?

SCHOOL!

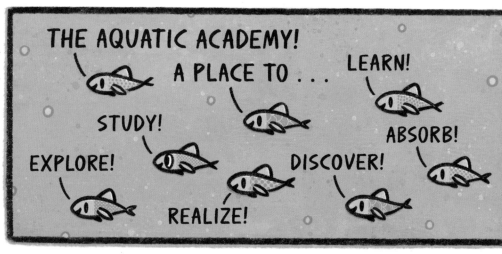

THE AQUATIC ACADEMY!

A PLACE TO . . .

LEARN!

STUDY!

ABSORB!

EXPLORE!

DISCOVER!

REALIZE!

OOO! COOL! I WANT TO COME TOO!

LET'S GO!

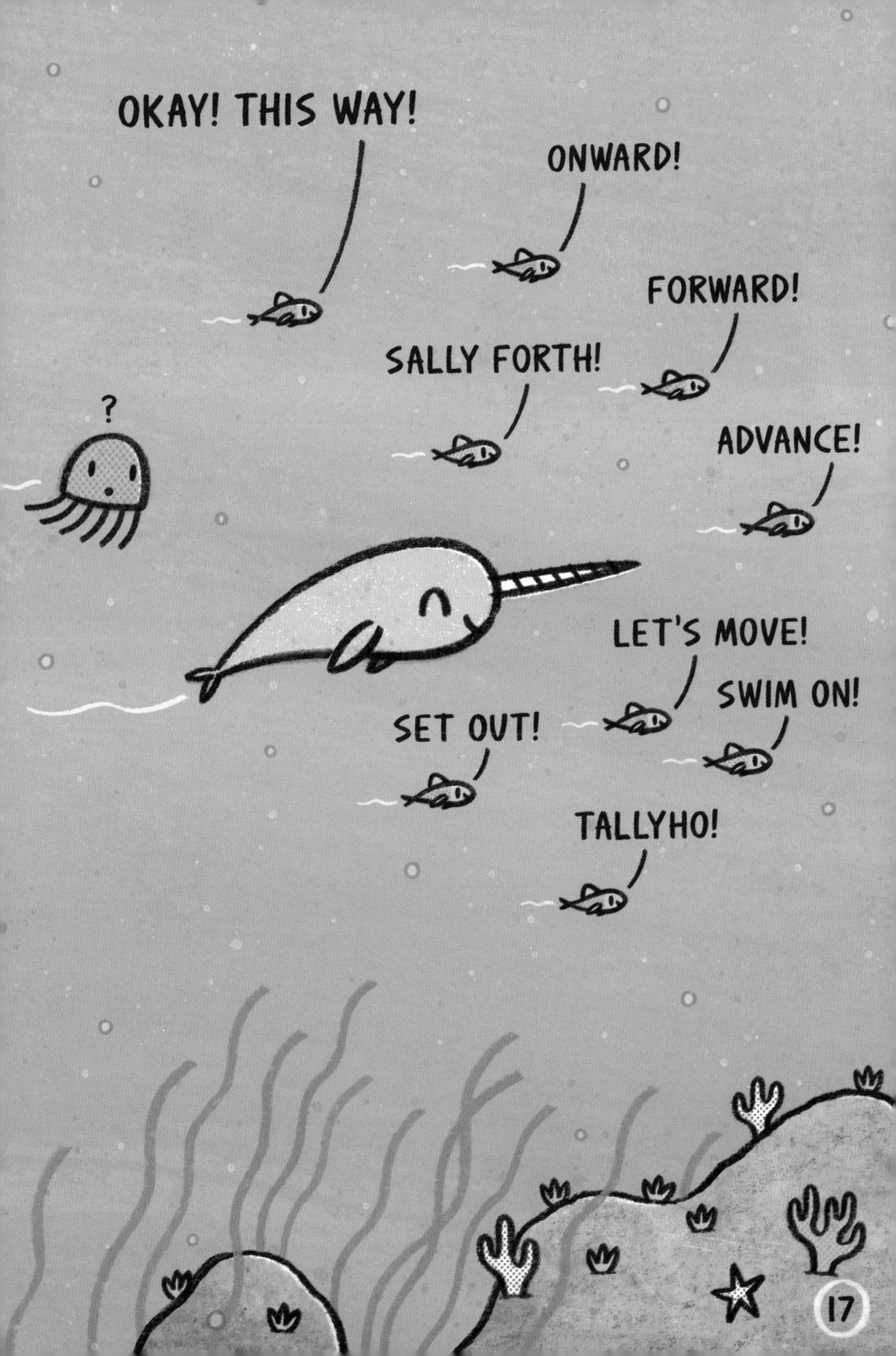
OKAY! THIS WAY!
ONWARD!
FORWARD!
SALLY FORTH!
?
ADVANCE!
LET'S MOVE!
SWIM ON!
SET OUT!
TALLYHO!

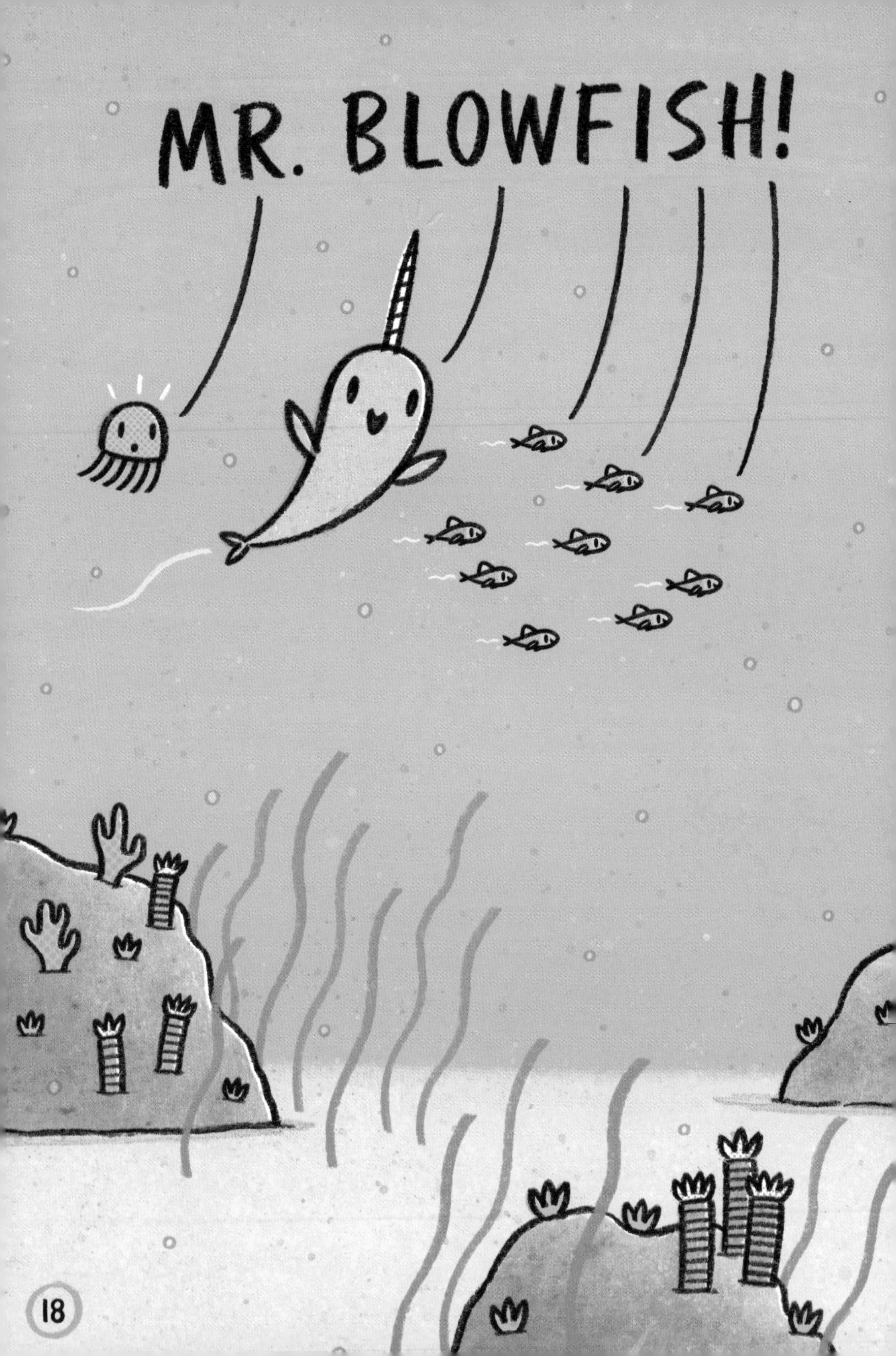
MR. BLOWFISH!

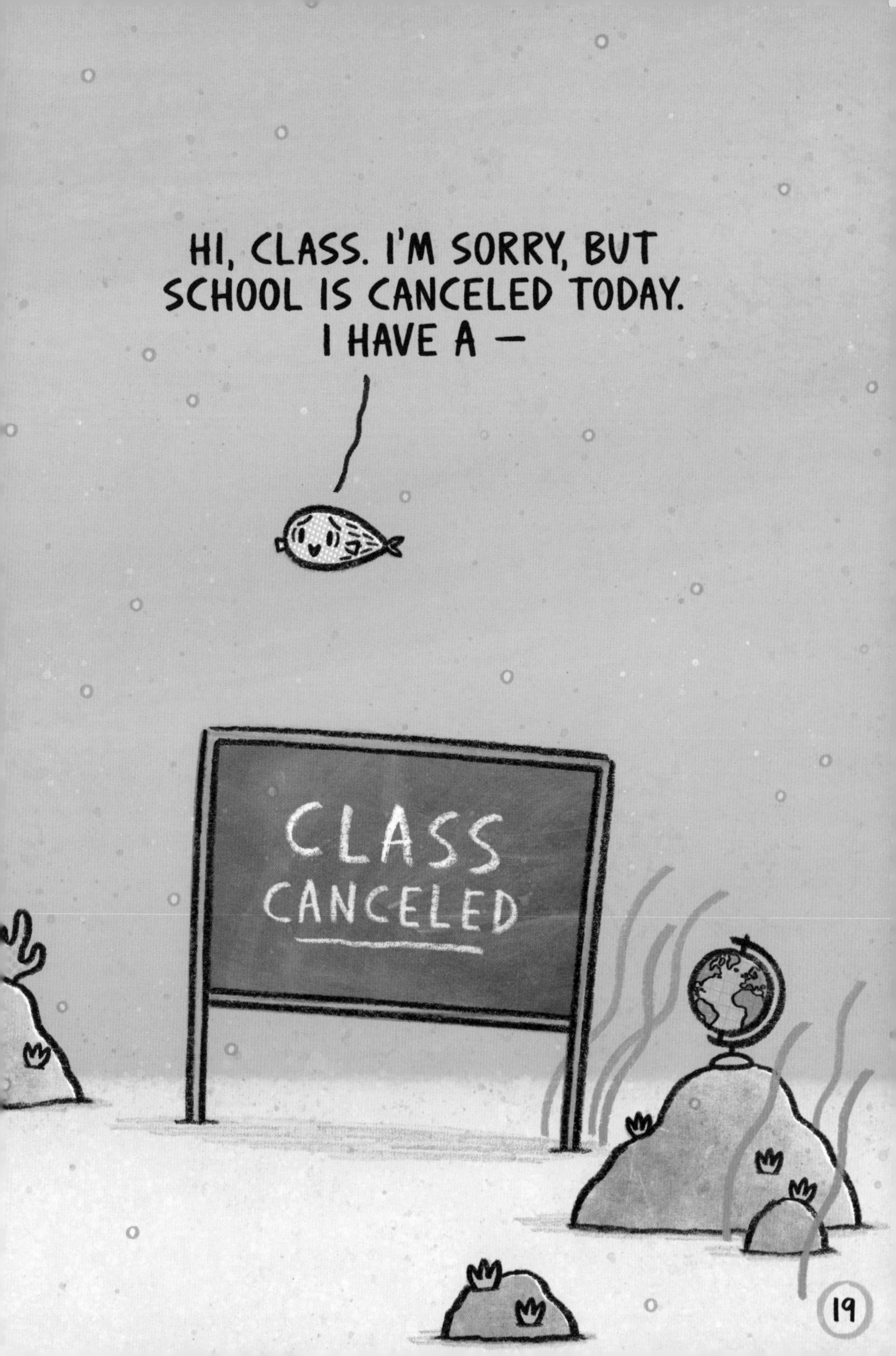
HI, CLASS. I'M SORRY, BUT SCHOOL IS CANCELED TODAY. I HAVE A —
CLASS CANCELED

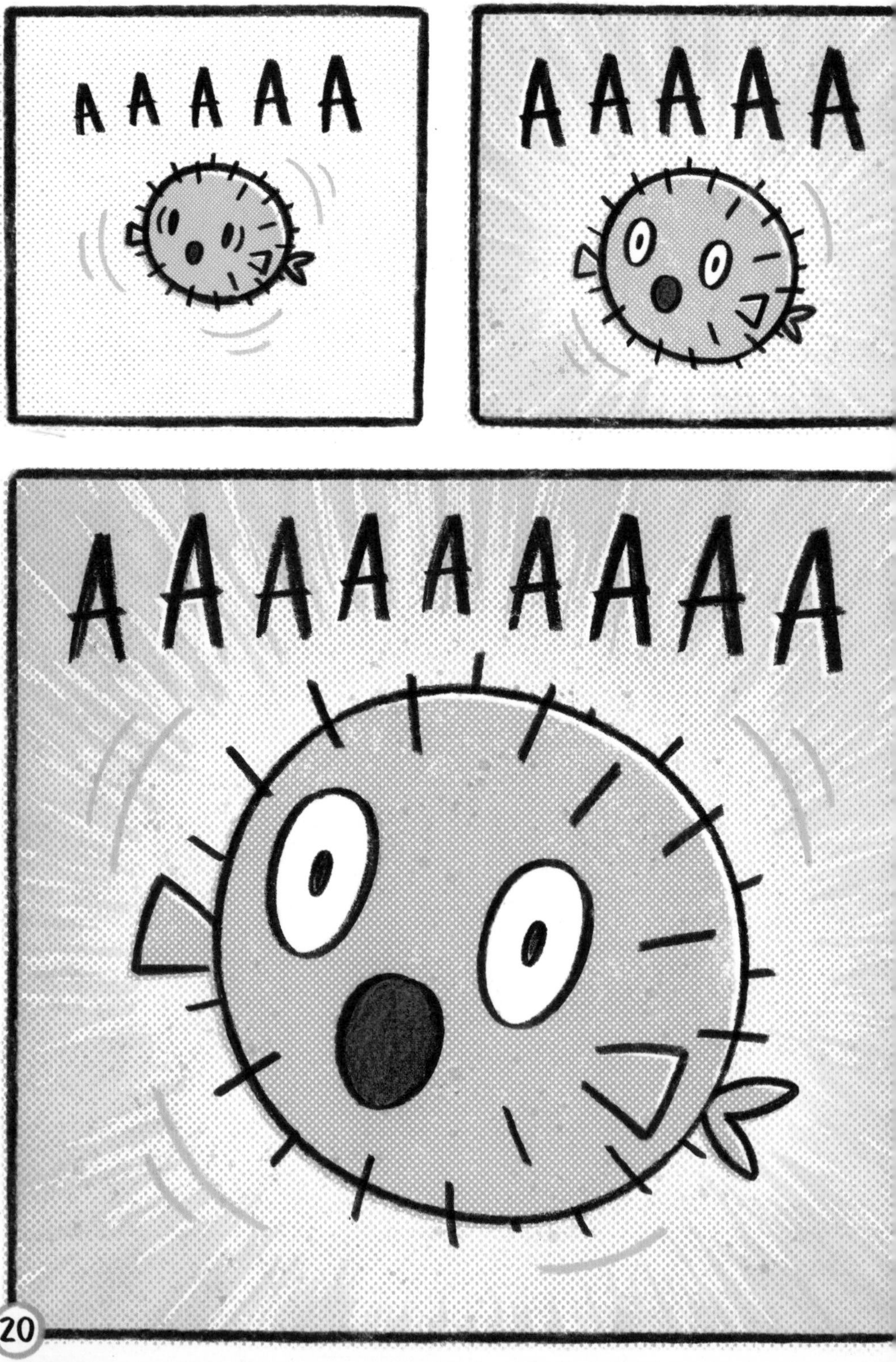
AAAAA
AAAAA
AAAAAAAAA

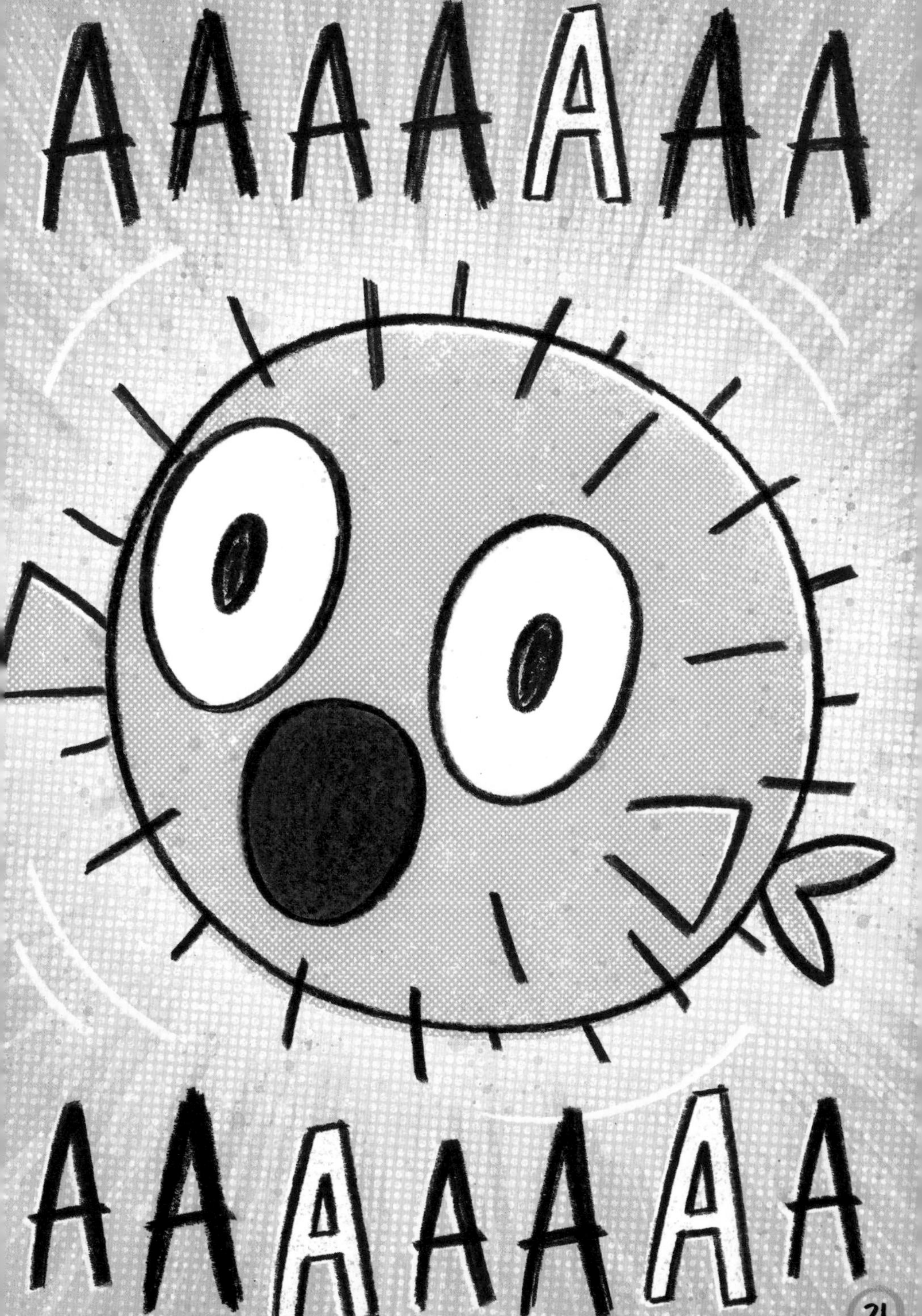
AAAAAAA
AAAAAAA

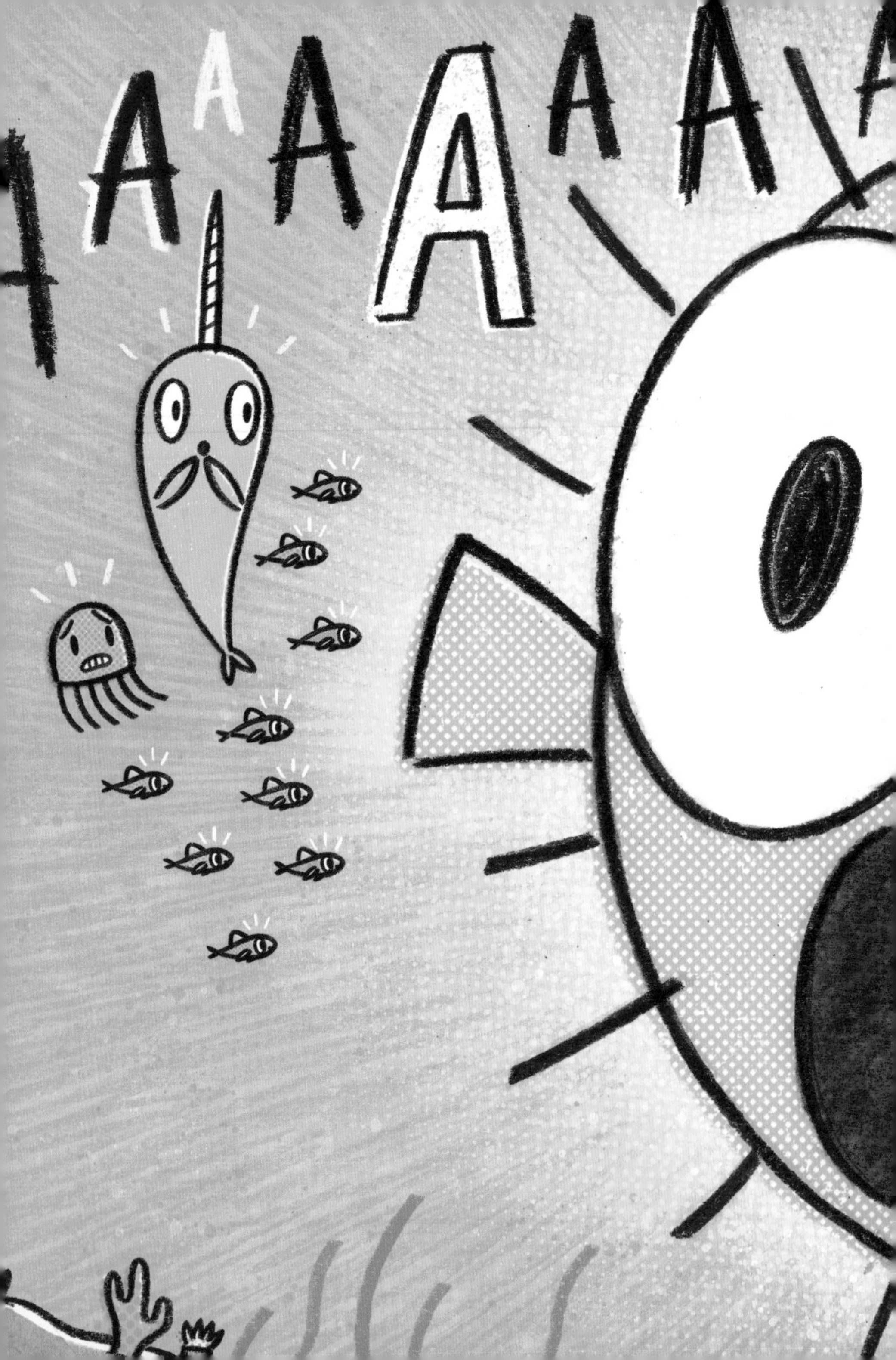
AAAAAA

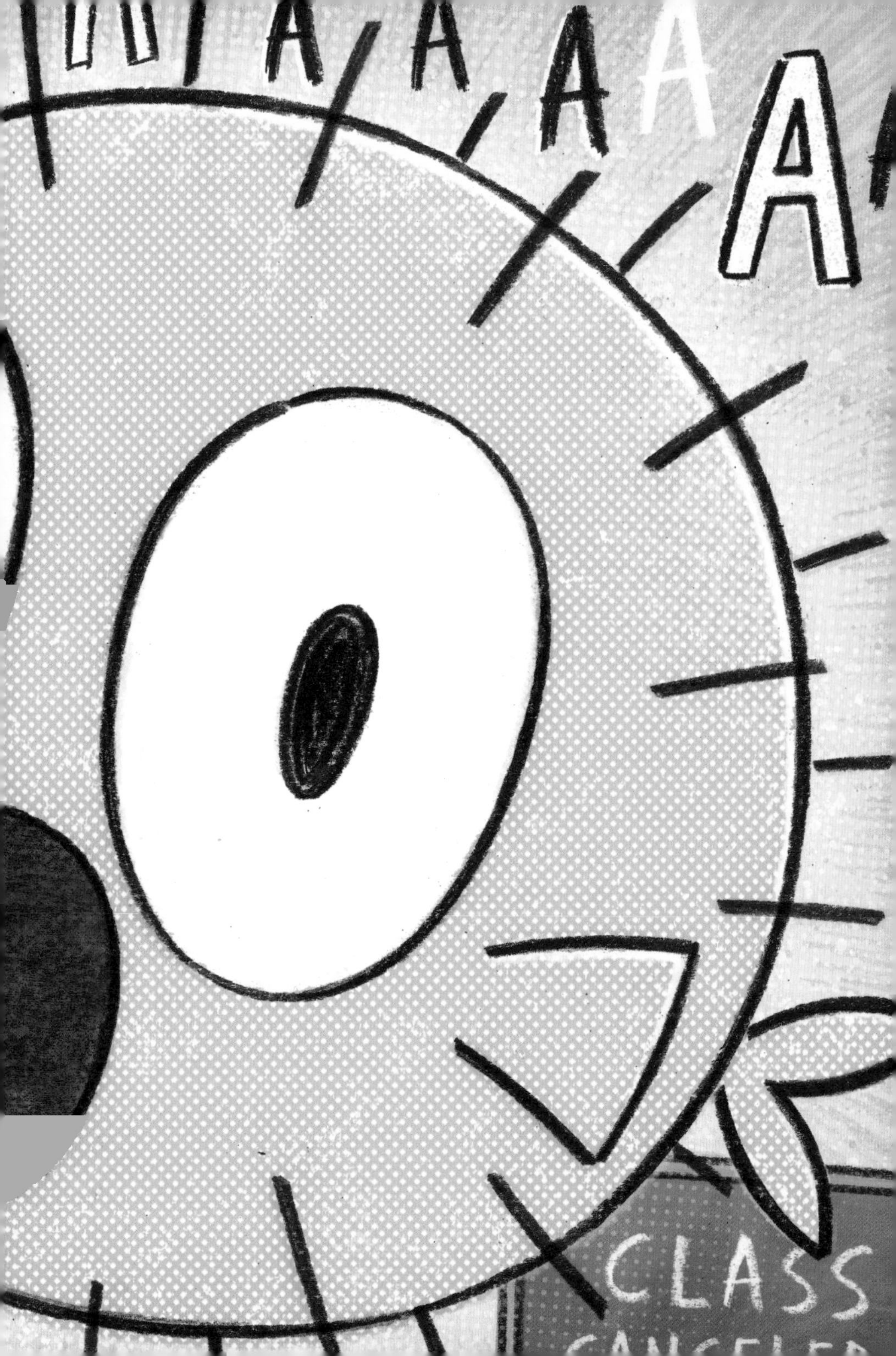
AAAAA
CLASS

CHOOOOOOOOOOOOOOOOOOOOOOOOOOOOOO

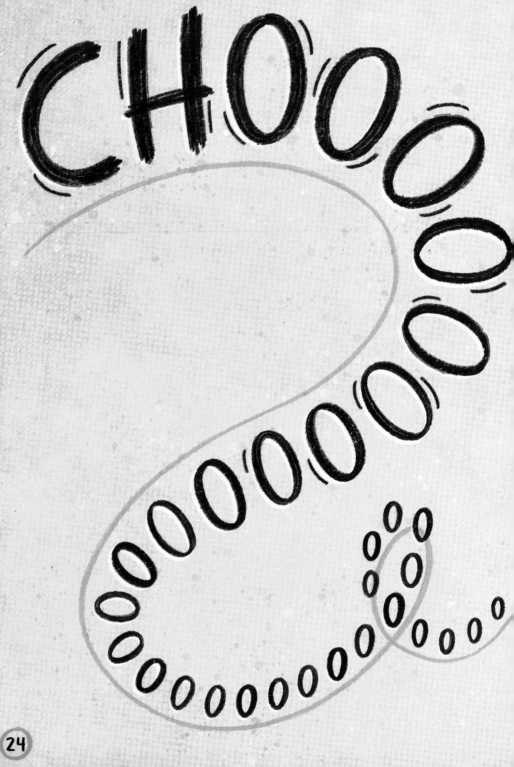

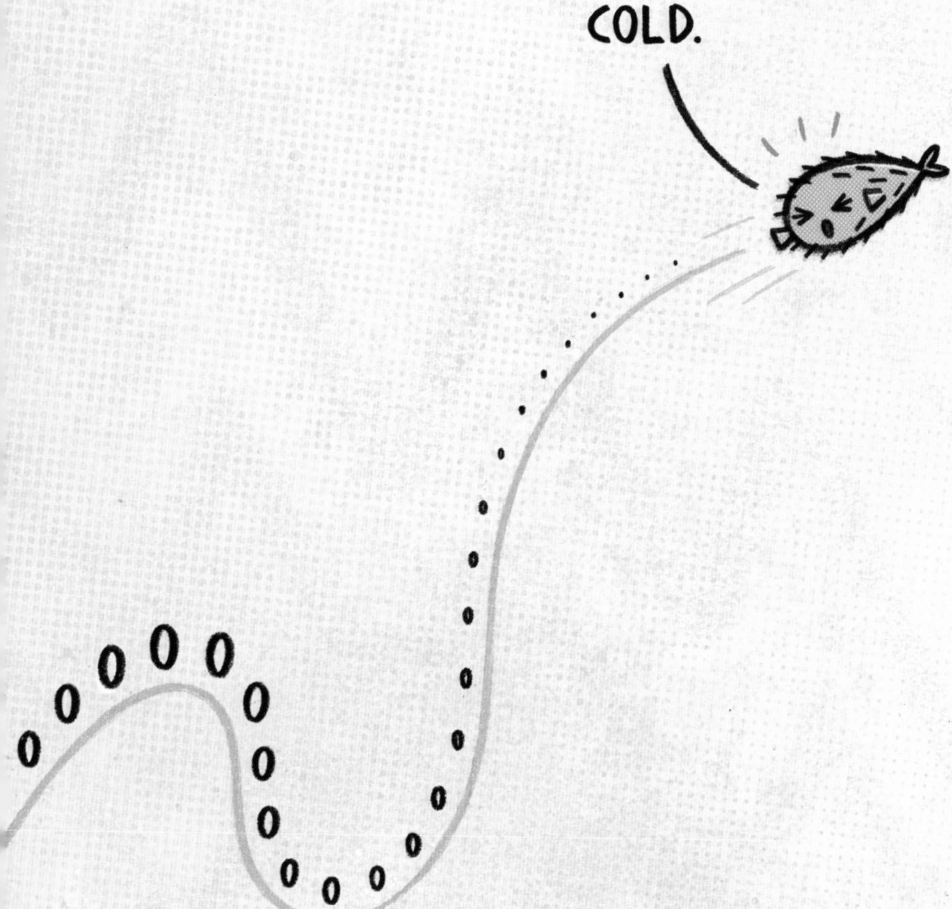
COLD.

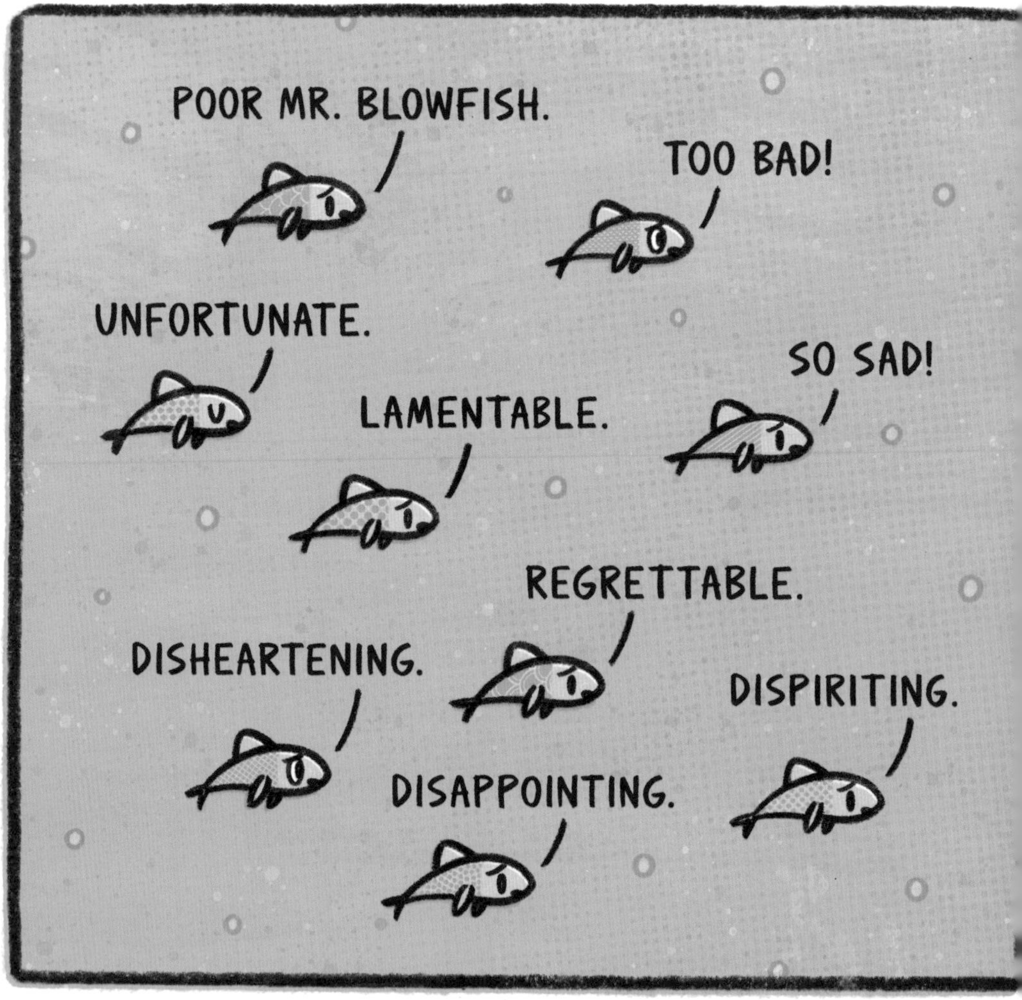
POOR MR. BLOWFISH.
TOO BAD!
UNFORTUNATE.
SO SAD!
LAMENTABLE.
REGRETTABLE.
DISHEARTENING.
DISPIRITING.
DISAPPOINTING.

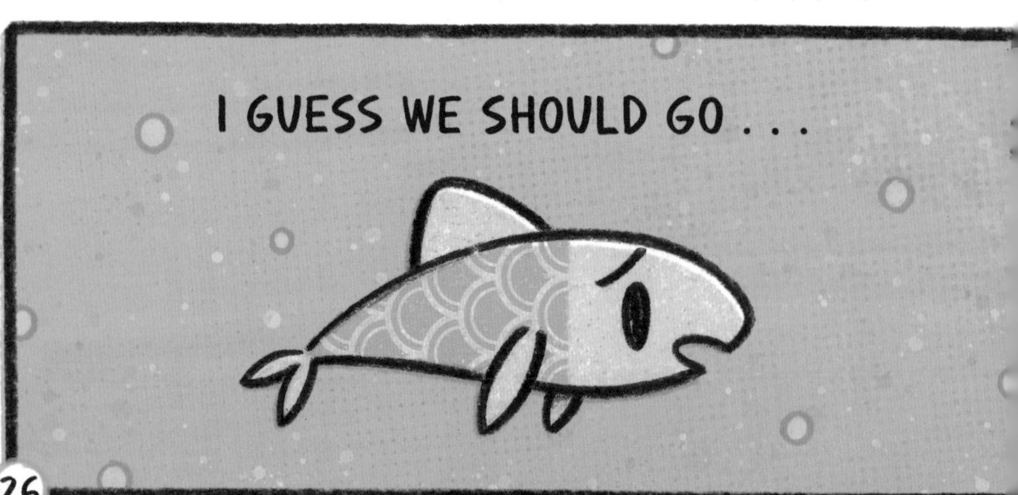
I GUESS WE SHOULD GO . . .

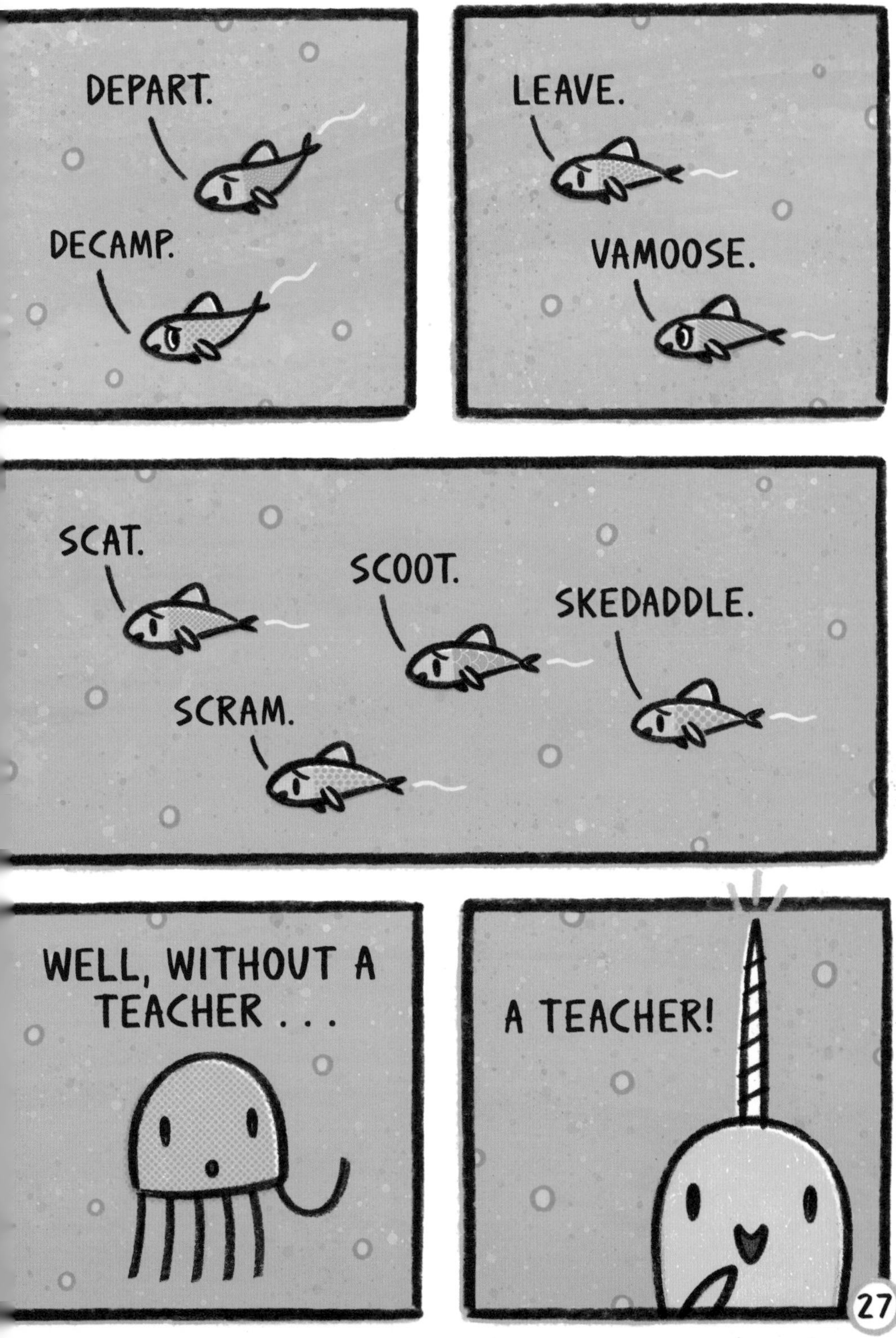

DEPART.
DECAMP.
LEAVE.
VAMOOSE.
SCAT.
SCOOT.
SKEDADDLE.
SCRAM.
WELL, WITHOUT A TEACHER . . .
A TEACHER!

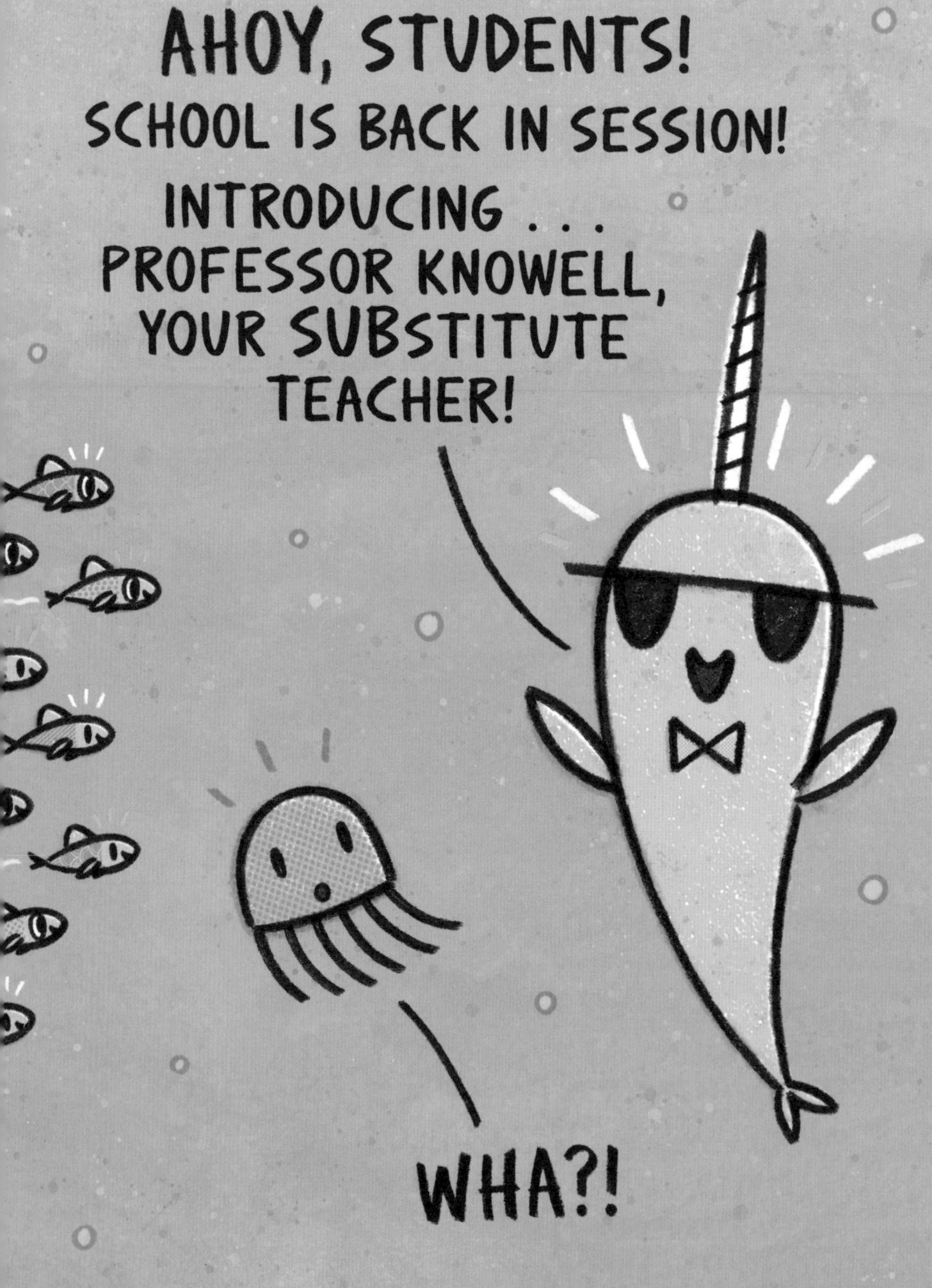
AHOY, STUDENTS!
SCHOOL IS BACK IN SESSION!
INTRODUCING . . . PROFESSOR KNOWELL, YOUR SUBSTITUTE TEACHER!
WHA?!

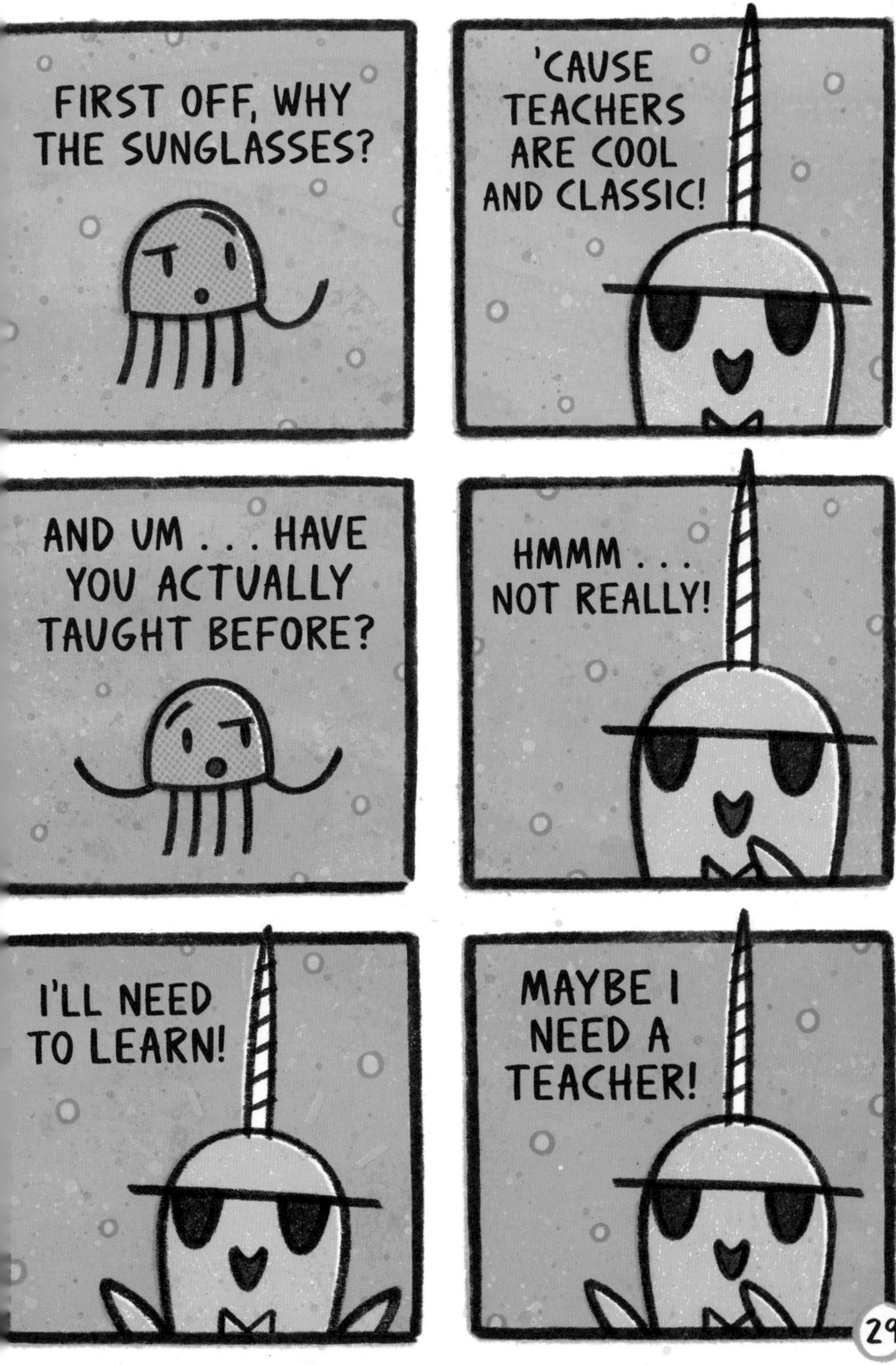
FIRST OFF, WHY THE SUNGLASSES?
'CAUSE TEACHERS ARE COOL AND CLASSIC!
AND UM . . . HAVE YOU ACTUALLY TAUGHT BEFORE?
HMMM . . . NOT REALLY!
I'LL NEED TO LEARN!
MAYBE I NEED A TEACHER!

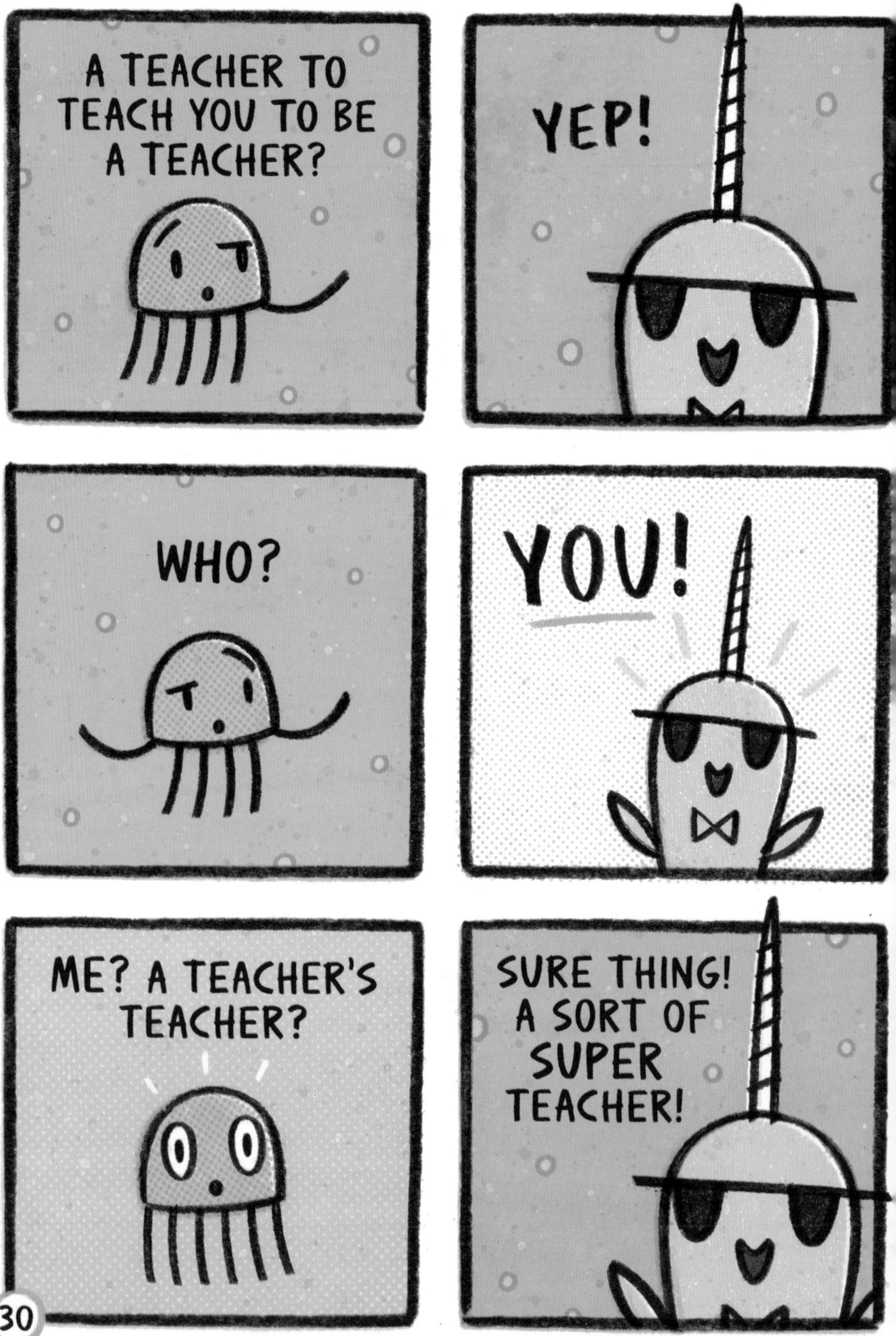
A TEACHER TO TEACH YOU TO BE A TEACHER?
YEP!
WHO?
YOU!
ME? A TEACHER'S TEACHER?
SURE THING! A SORT OF SUPER TEACHER!

A SUPER TEACHER?

PRETTY MUCH!

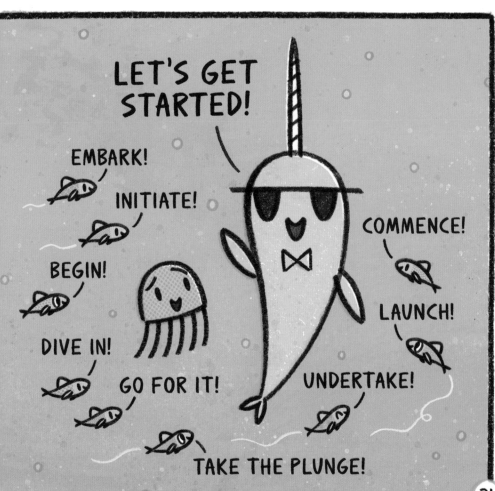

LET'S GET STARTED!

EMBARK!

INITIATE!

BEGIN!

DIVE IN!

GO FOR IT!

COMMENCE!

LAUNCH!

UNDERTAKE!

TAKE THE PLUNGE!

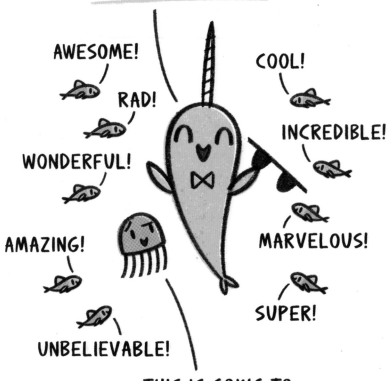

THIS IS GOING TO BE
FINTASTIC!

AWESOME!

COOL!

RAD!

INCREDIBLE!

WONDERFUL!

AMAZING!

MARVELOUS!

SUPER!

UNBELIEVABLE!

THIS IS GOING TO
BE . . . SOMETHING.

A GREAT GROUP OF FUN FACTS

YOU PROBABLY ALREADY KNOW THAT A GROUP OF CHICKENS IS CALLED A FLOCK AND A GROUP OF DEER IS COMMONLY CALLED A HERD. BUT HAVE YOU HEARD OF A TOWER OF GIRAFFES OR A BLOAT OF HIPPOS? MANY SEA CREATURES HAVE FUN GROUP NAMES TOO!

NEAT!

FASCINATING!

CAPTIVATING!

INTERESTING!

A GROUP OF FISH ALL THE SAME SPECIES AND SWIMMING IN SYNC IS KNOWN AS A SCHOOL. THE SIZE AND SYNCHRONIZED MOVEMENTS OF A SCHOOL OF FISH CAN CONFUSE AND EVEN SCARE PREDATORS.

EEP! MONSTER!

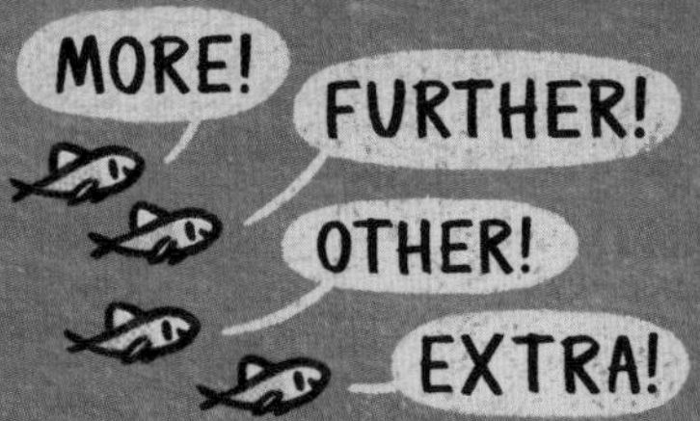
MORE!
FURTHER!
OTHER!
EXTRA!

FUN FACTS

A GROUP OF SEA SNAILS IS CALLED A WALK.

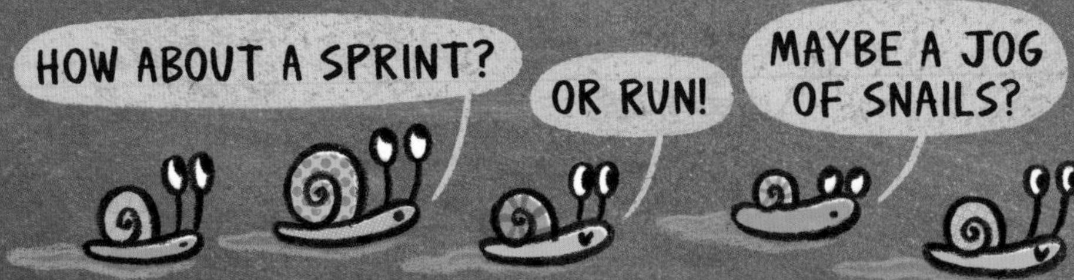
HOW ABOUT A SPRINT?
OR RUN!
MAYBE A JOG OF SNAILS?

A GROUP OF OYSTERS IS CALLED A BED.

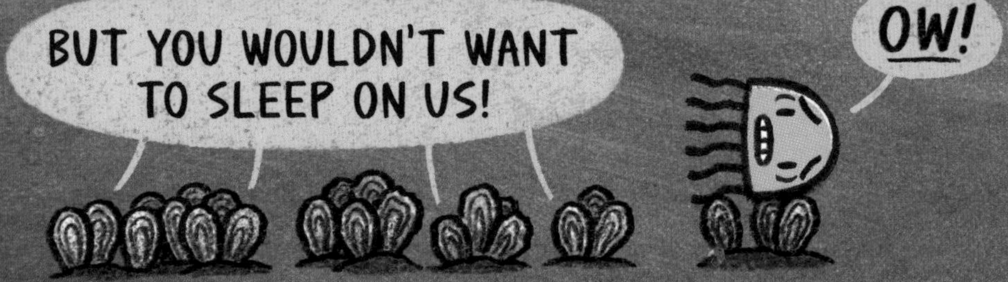
BUT YOU WOULDN'T WANT TO SLEEP ON US!
OW!

A GROUP OF SHARKS IS OFTEN CALLED A SHIVER.

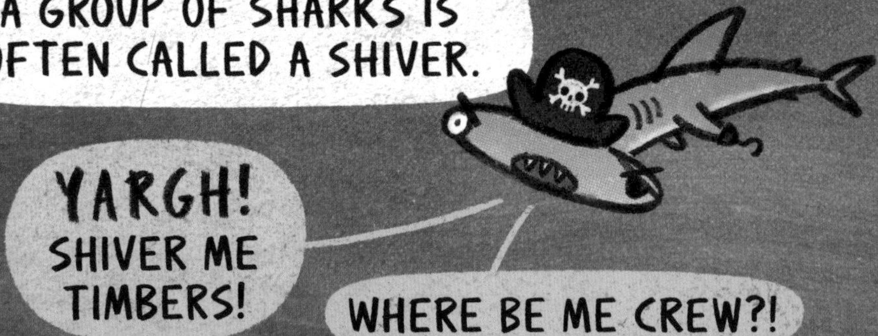
YARGH! SHIVER ME TIMBERS!
WHERE BE ME CREW?!

WAFFLEMATICS

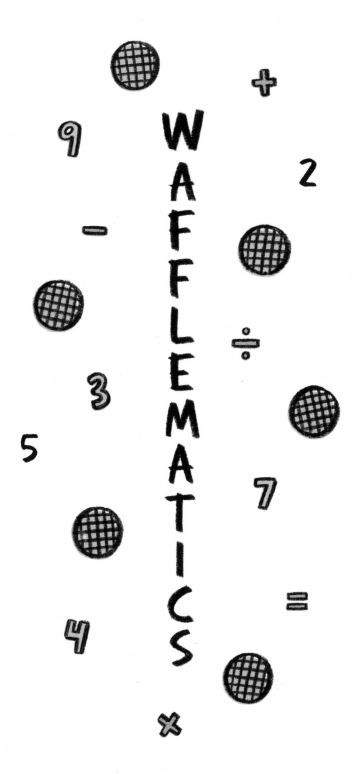

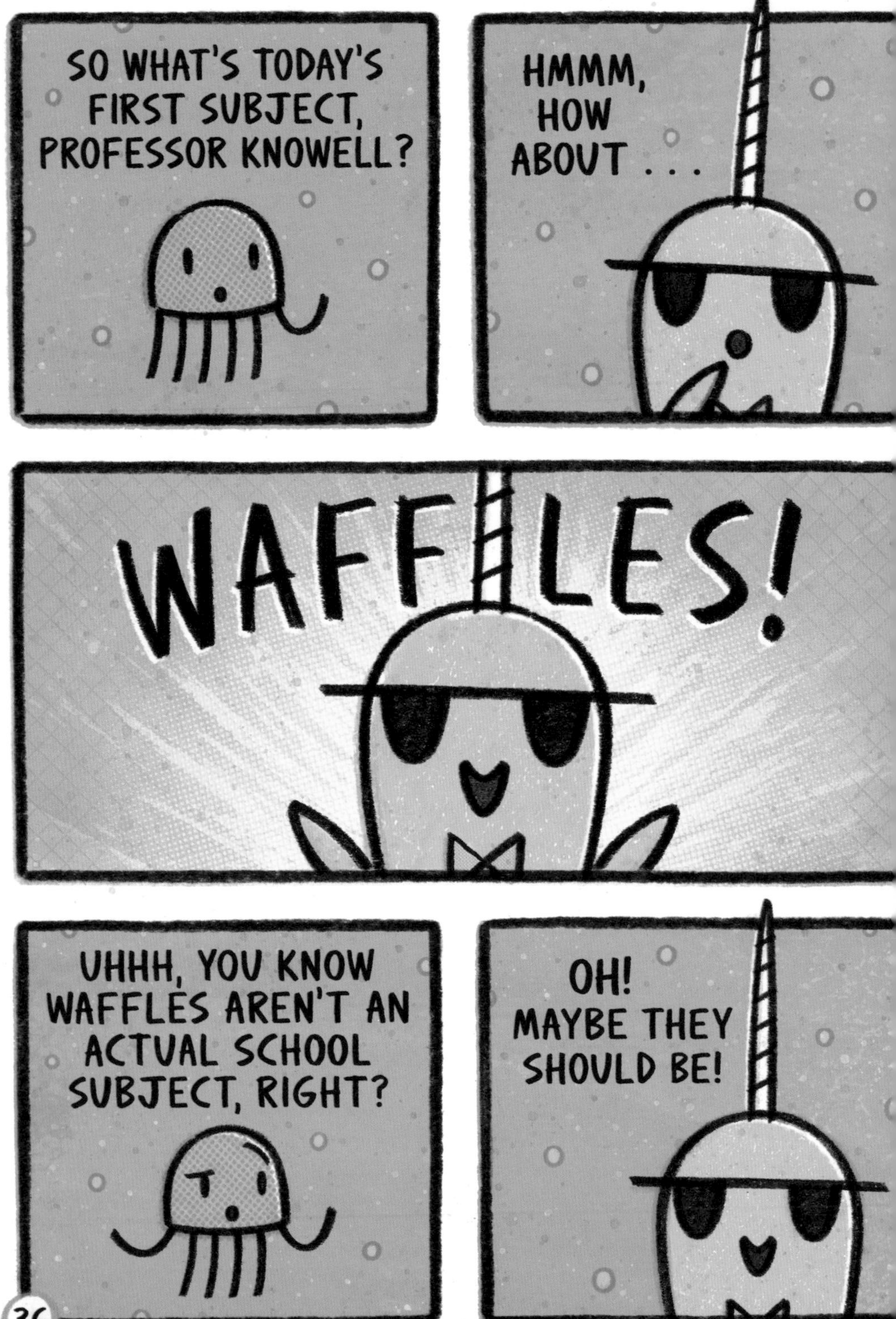
SO WHAT'S TODAY'S FIRST SUBJECT, PROFESSOR KNOWELL?
HMMM, HOW ABOUT . . .
WAFFLES!
UHHH, YOU KNOW WAFFLES AREN'T AN ACTUAL SCHOOL SUBJECT, RIGHT?
OH! MAYBE THEY SHOULD BE!

HOW ABOUT SOMETHING FUNDAMENTAL . . . LIKE MATHEMATICS?

FUNDAMENTAL? OOOOOOO! LET'S STUDY . . .

WAFFLEMATICS!

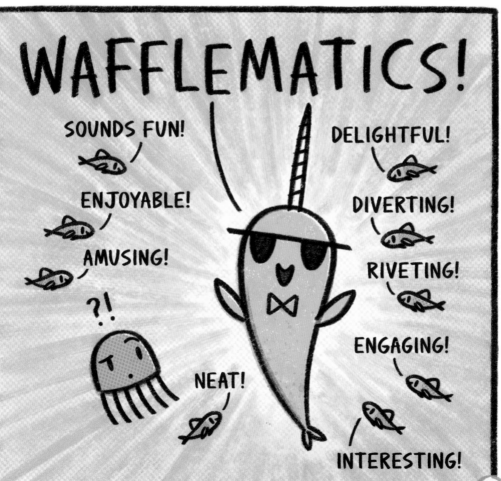

SOUNDS FUN!

DELIGHTFUL!

ENJOYABLE!

DIVERTING!

AMUSING!

RIVETING!

?!

ENGAGING!

NEAT!

INTERESTING!

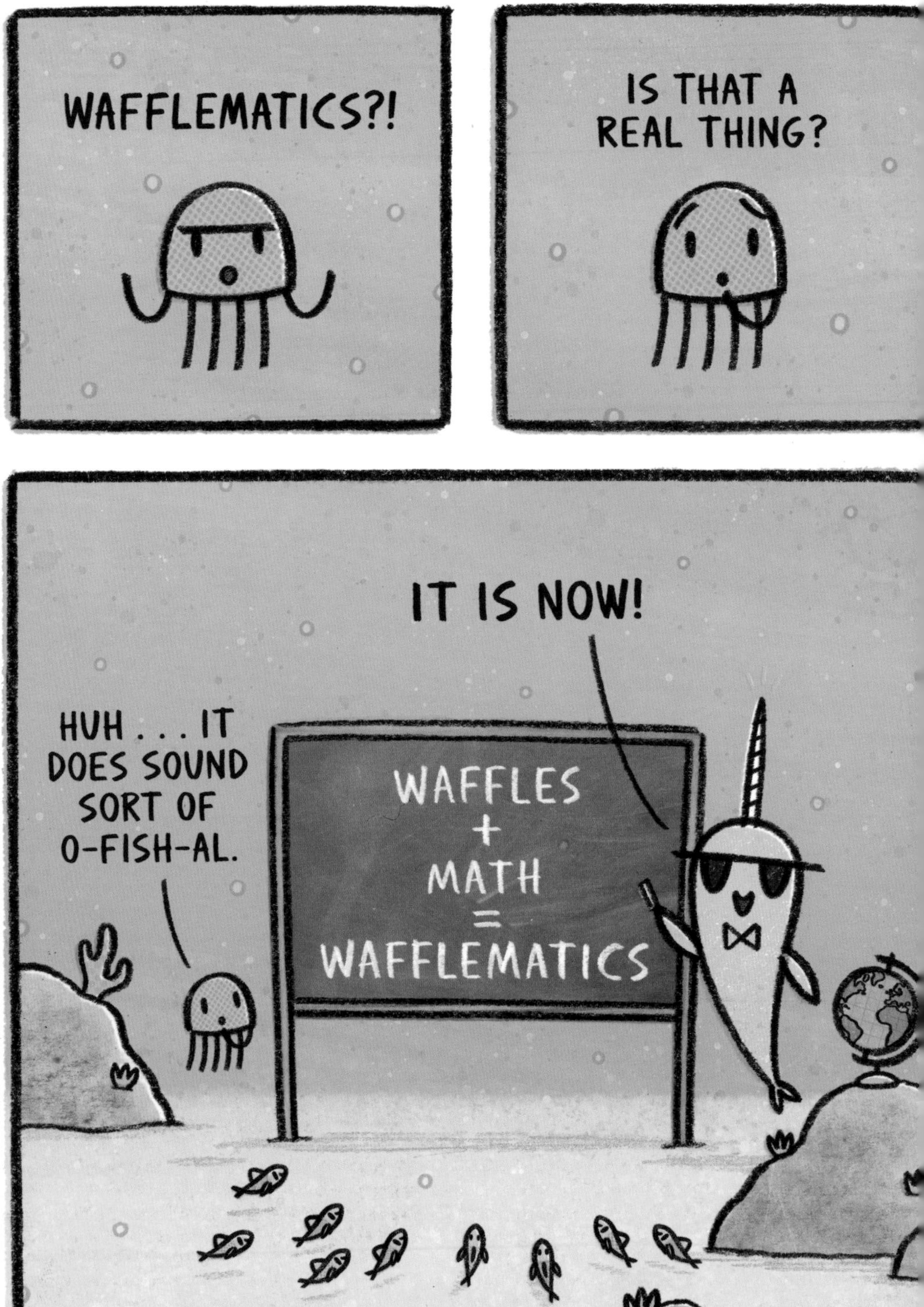
WAFFLEMATICS?!
IS THAT A REAL THING?
IT IS NOW!
WAFFLES + MATH = WAFFLEMATICS
HUH . . . IT DOES SOUND SORT OF O-FISH-AL.

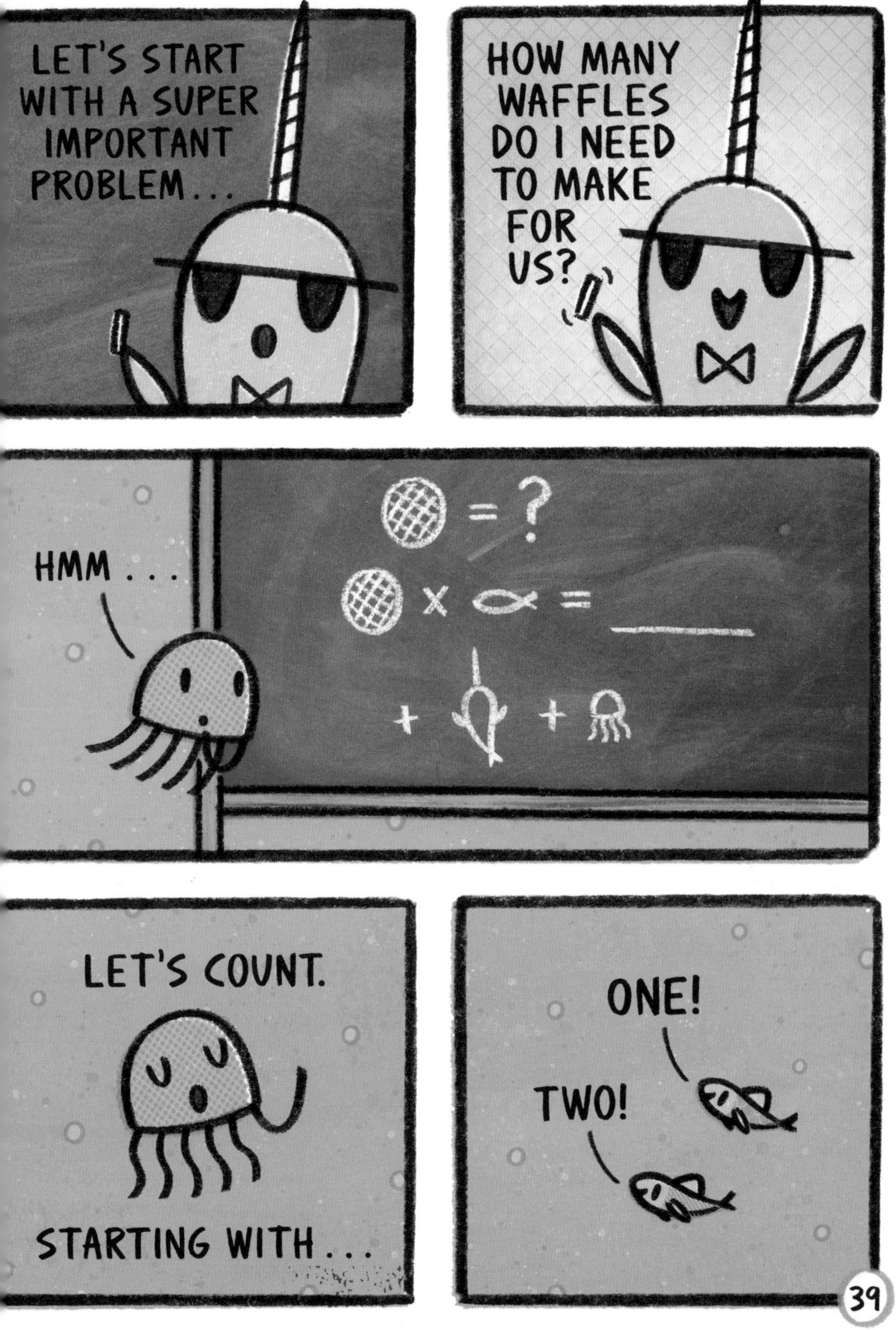
LET'S START WITH A SUPER IMPORTANT PROBLEM...
HOW MANY WAFFLES DO I NEED TO MAKE FOR US?
HMM...
LET'S COUNT.
STARTING WITH...
ONE!
TWO!

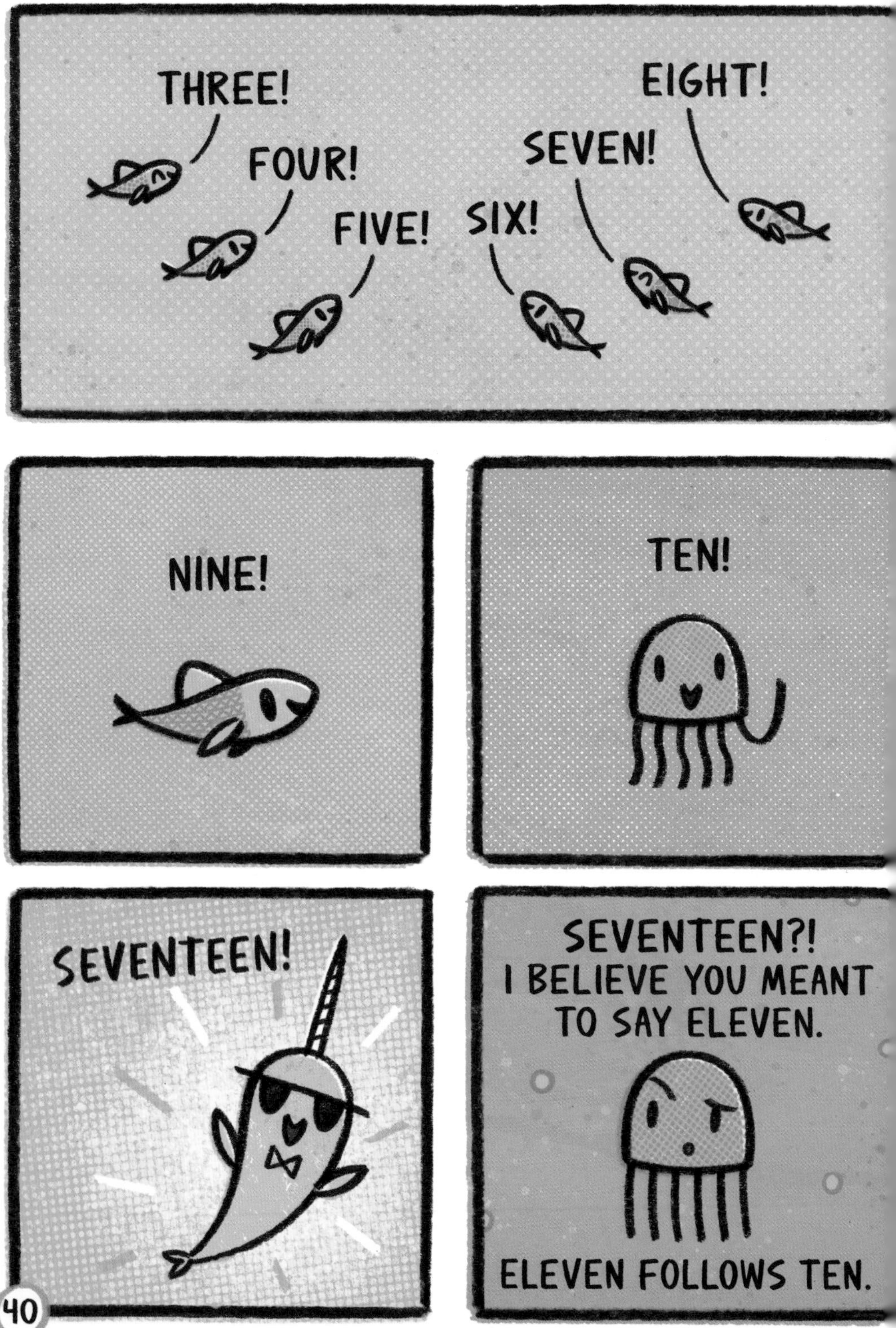

THREE!
FOUR!
FIVE!
SIX!
SEVEN!
EIGHT!
NINE!
TEN!
SEVENTEEN!
SEVENTEEN?! I BELIEVE YOU MEANT TO SAY ELEVEN.
ELEVEN FOLLOWS TEN.

TRUE! BUT I WANT TO EAT AT LEAST SEVEN WAFFLES!

OH! I'D LIKE TWO ACTUALLY!

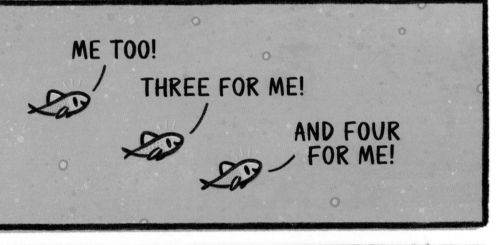

ME TOO!

THREE FOR ME!

AND FOUR FOR ME!

THIS IS WHAT I'M CHALKING ABOUT! THIS IS ADDING UP TO OODLES OF WAFFLES!

$7 + 2 + 2 + 3 + 4$

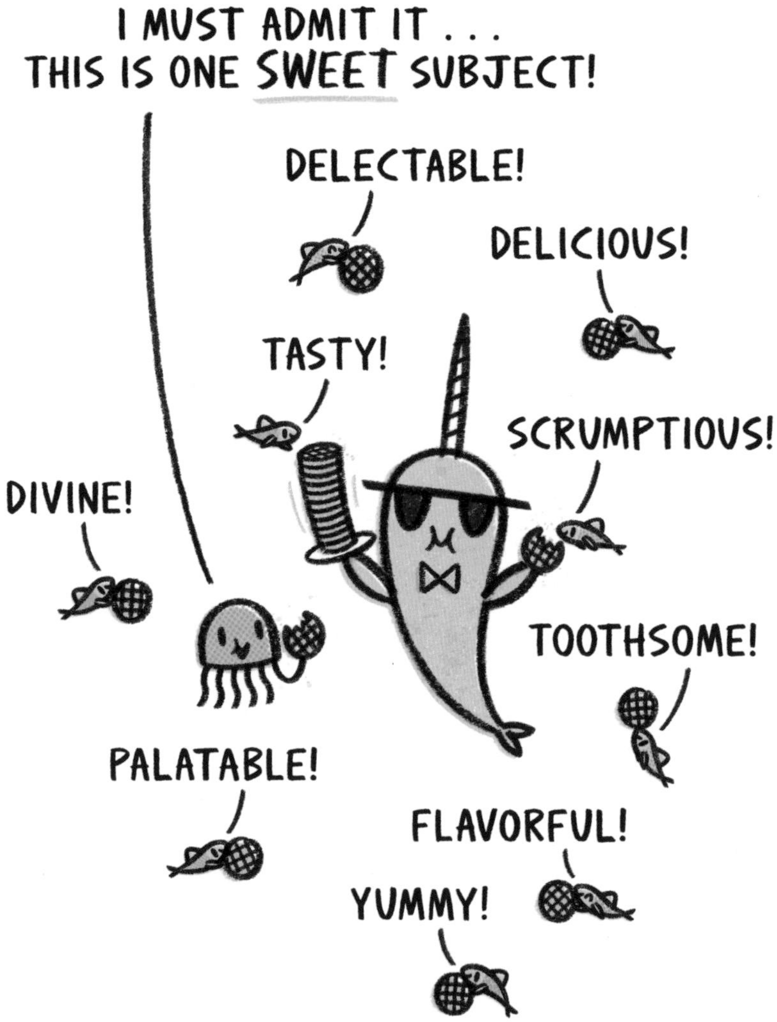
I MUST ADMIT IT . . .
THIS IS ONE SWEET SUBJECT!
DELECTABLE!
DELICIOUS!
TASTY!
SCRUMPTIOUS!
DIVINE!
TOOTHSOME!
PALATABLE!
FLAVORFUL!
YUMMY!

SCIENCE SQUAD

SQUAD

VS.

FUN

FINDERS

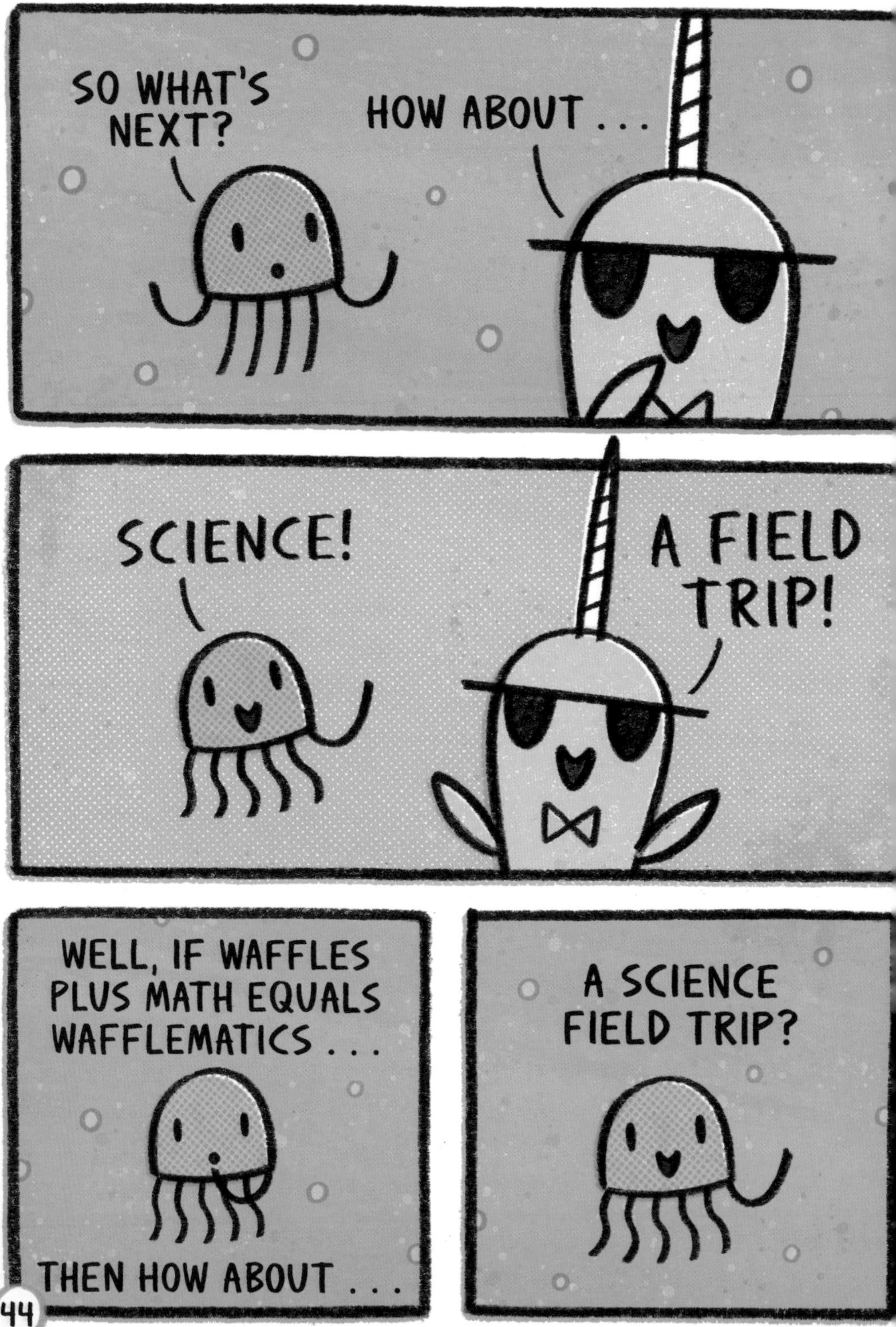

SO WHAT'S NEXT?
HOW ABOUT . . .
SCIENCE!
A FIELD TRIP!
WELL, IF WAFFLES PLUS MATH EQUALS WAFFLEMATICS . . .
THEN HOW ABOUT . . .
A SCIENCE FIELD TRIP?

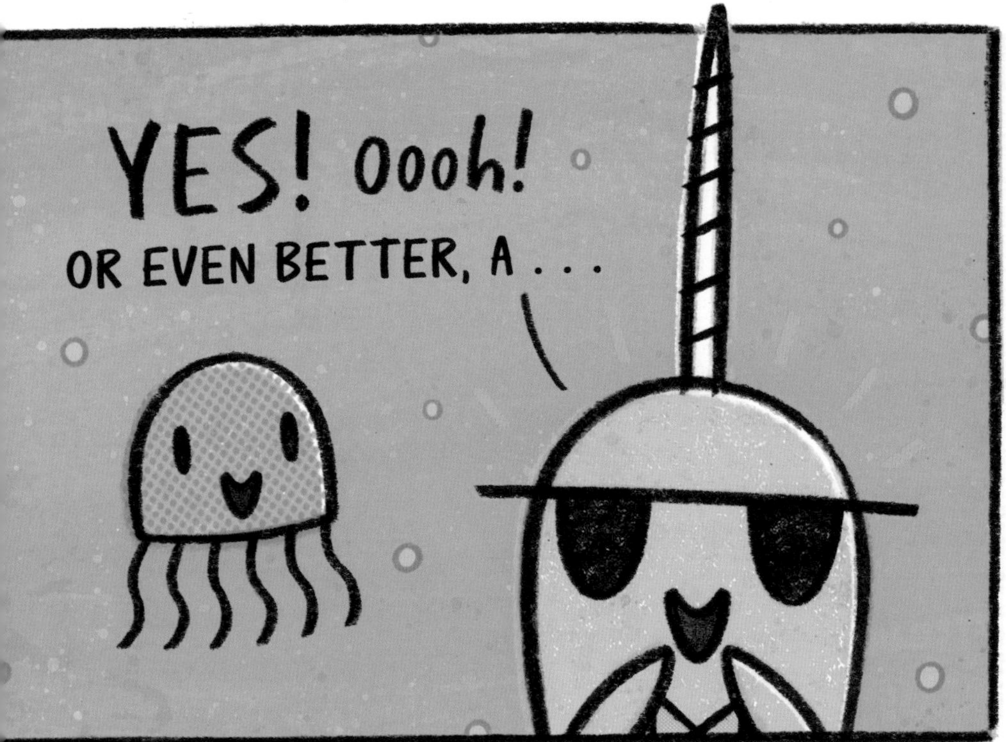
YES! Oooh!
OR EVEN BETTER, A . . .

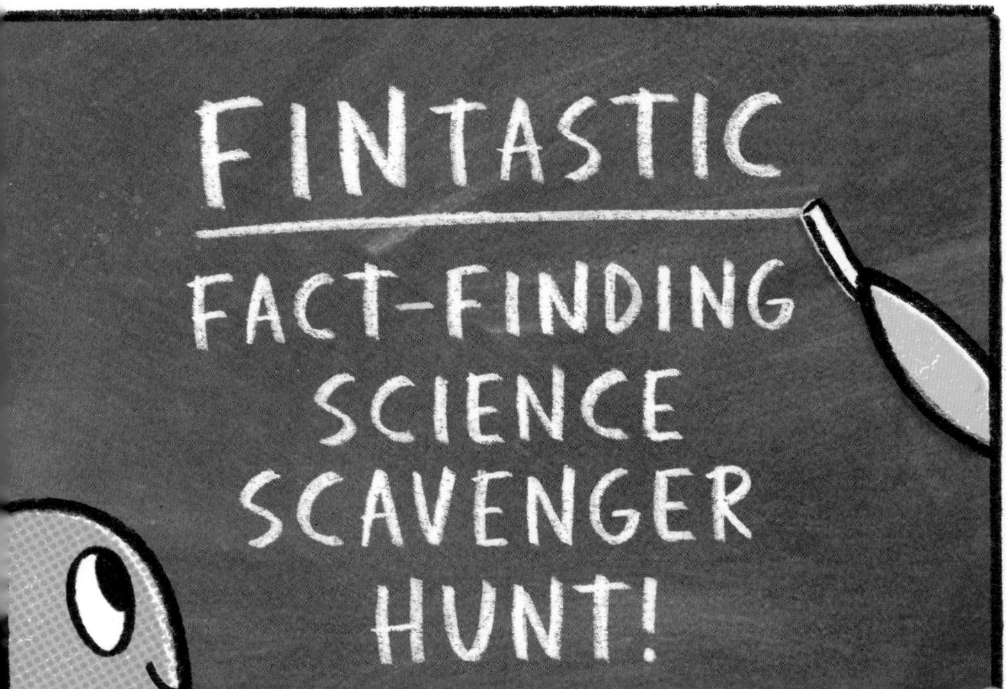
FINTASTIC
FACT-FINDING
SCIENCE
SCAVENGER
HUNT!

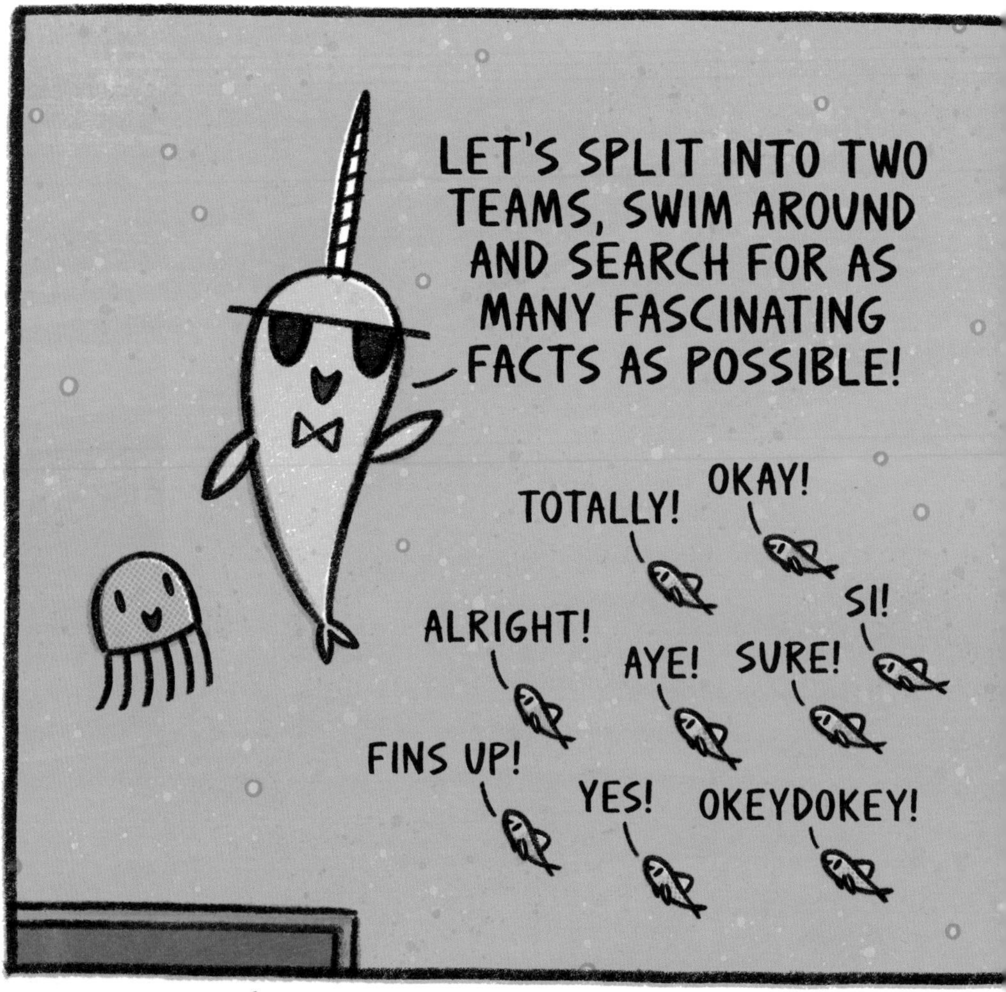
LET'S SPLIT INTO TWO TEAMS, SWIM AROUND AND SEARCH FOR AS MANY FASCINATING FACTS AS POSSIBLE!
TOTALLY!
OKAY!
SI!
ALRIGHT!
AYE!
SURE!
FINS UP!
YES!
OKEYDOKEY!

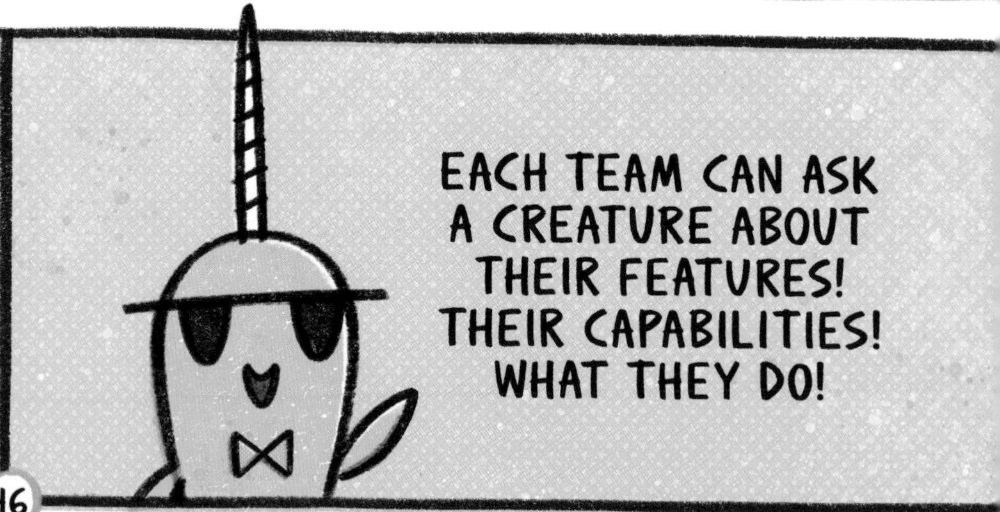
EACH TEAM CAN ASK A CREATURE ABOUT THEIR FEATURES! THEIR CAPABILITIES! WHAT THEY DO!

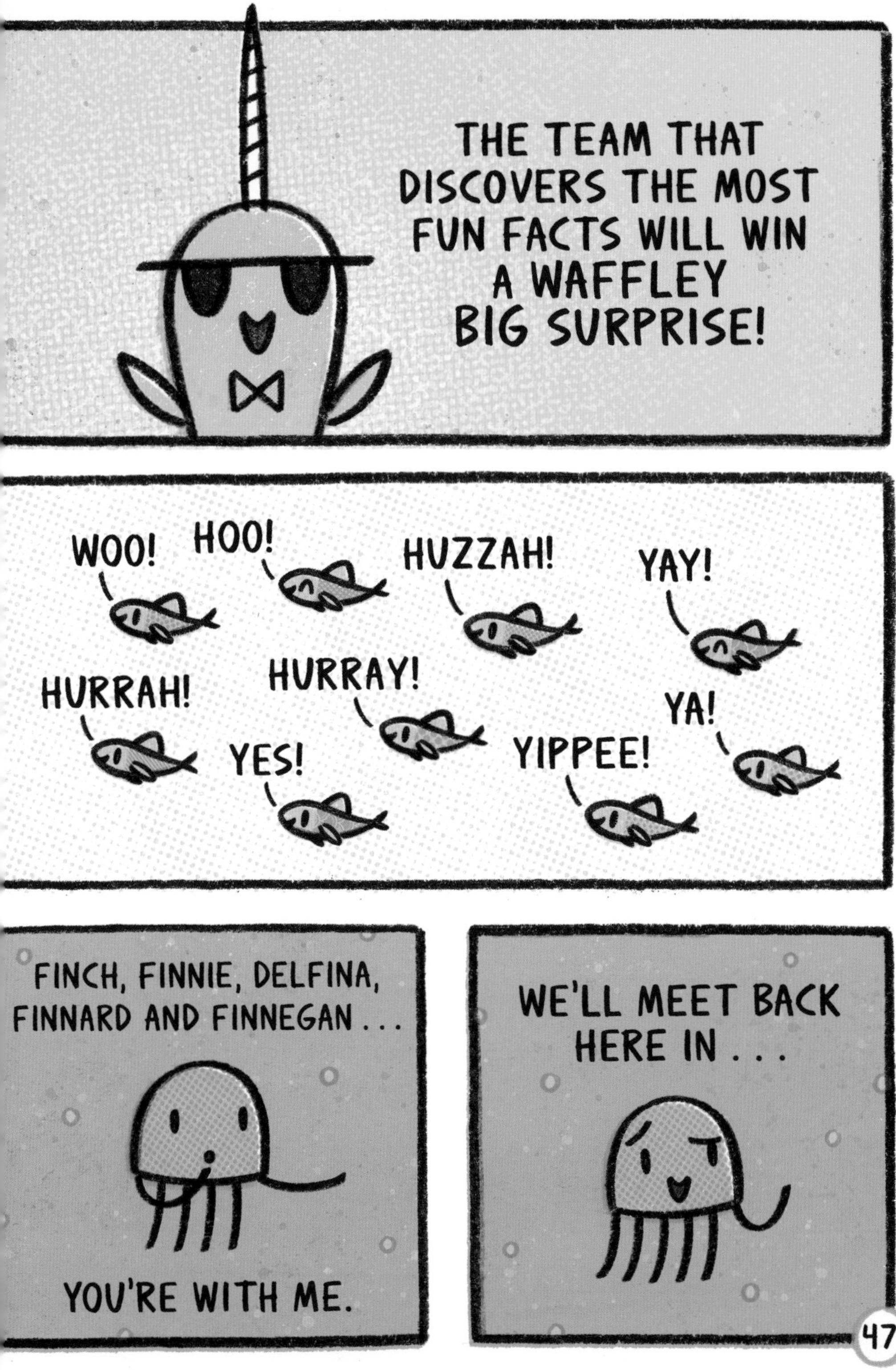
THE TEAM THAT DISCOVERS THE MOST FUN FACTS WILL WIN A WAFFLEY BIG SURPRISE!
WOO!
HOO!
HUZZAH!
YAY!
HURRAH!
HURRAY!
YA!
YES!
YIPPEE!
FINCH, FINNIE, DELFINA, FINNARD AND FINNEGAN . . .
YOU'RE WITH ME.
WE'LL MEET BACK HERE IN . . .

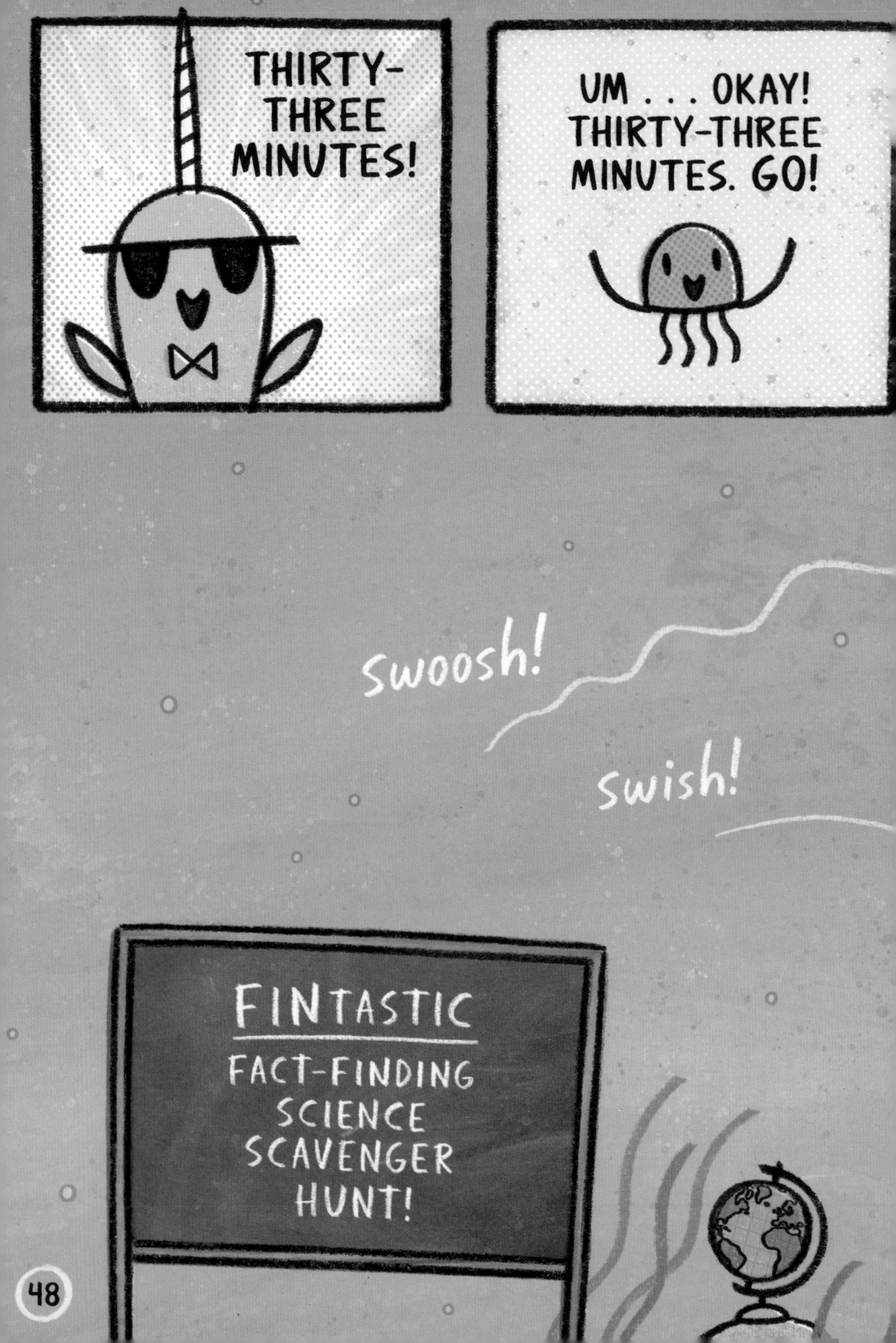
THIRTY-THREE MINUTES!
UM . . . OKAY! THIRTY-THREE MINUTES. GO!
swoosh!
swish!
FINTASTIC
FACT-FINDING SCIENCE SCAVENGER HUNT!

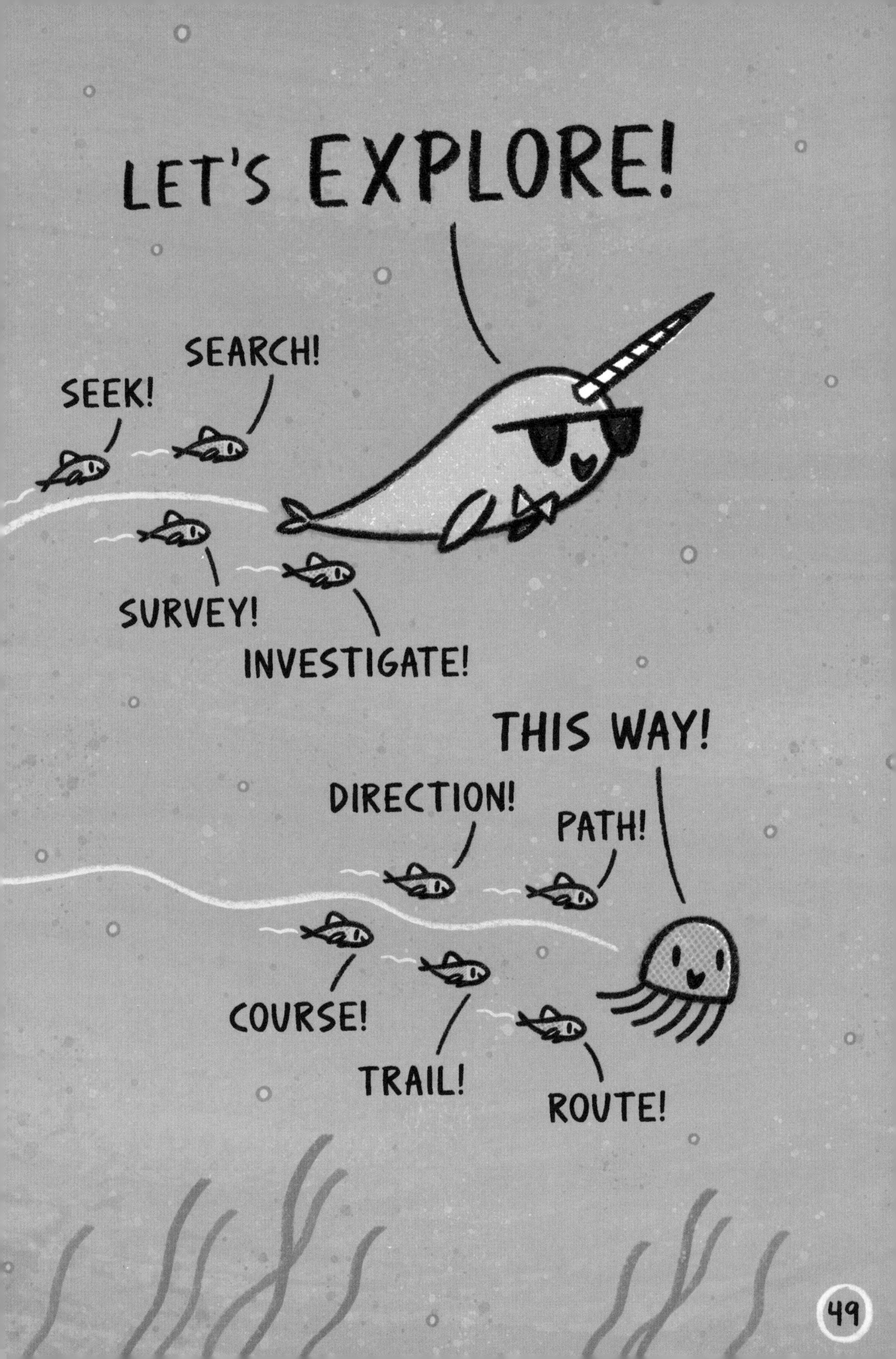
LET'S EXPLORE!
SEEK!
SEARCH!
SURVEY!
INVESTIGATE!
THIS WAY!
DIRECTION!
PATH!
COURSE!
TRAIL!
ROUTE!

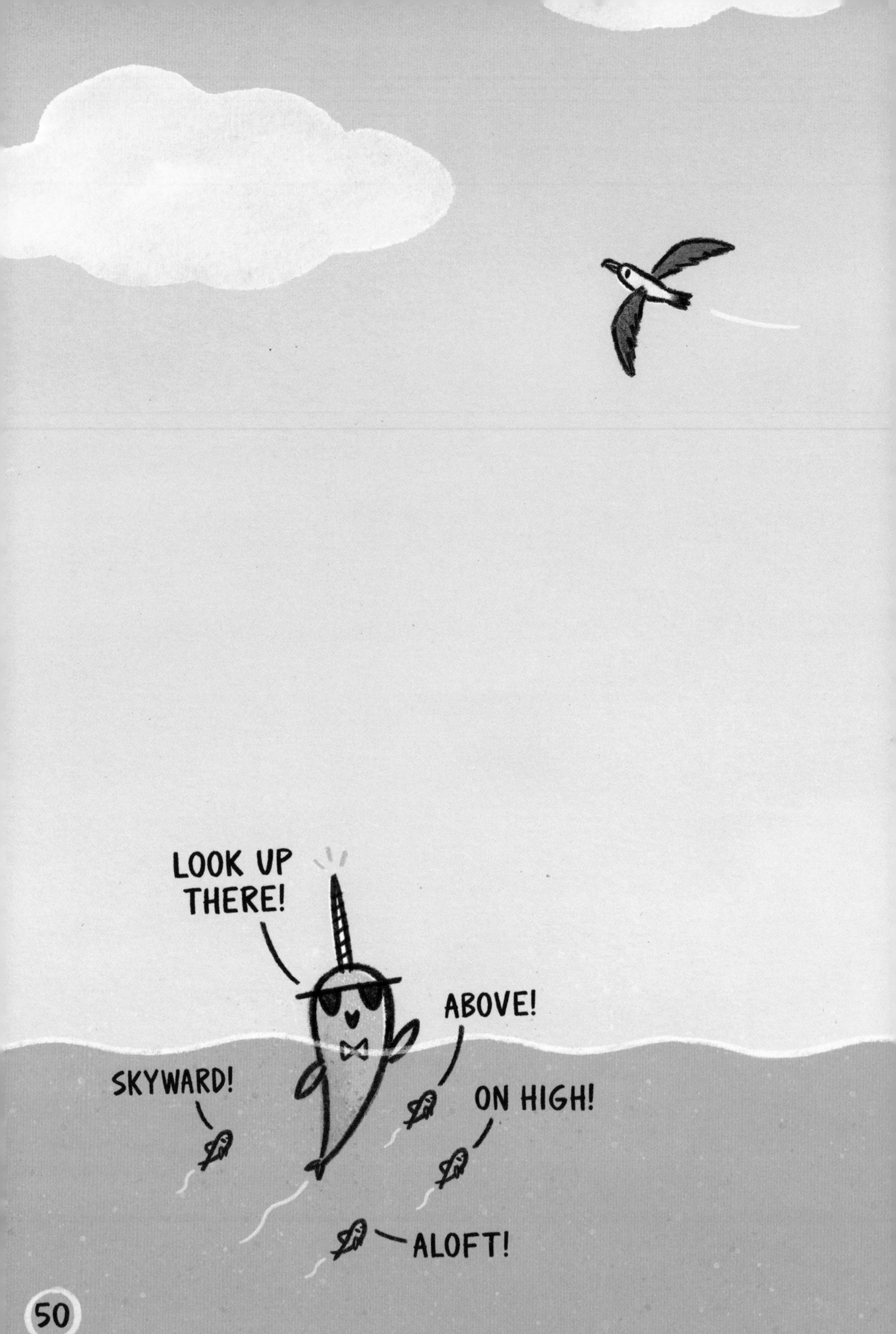
LOOK UP THERE!
ABOVE!
SKYWARD!
ON HIGH!
ALOFT!

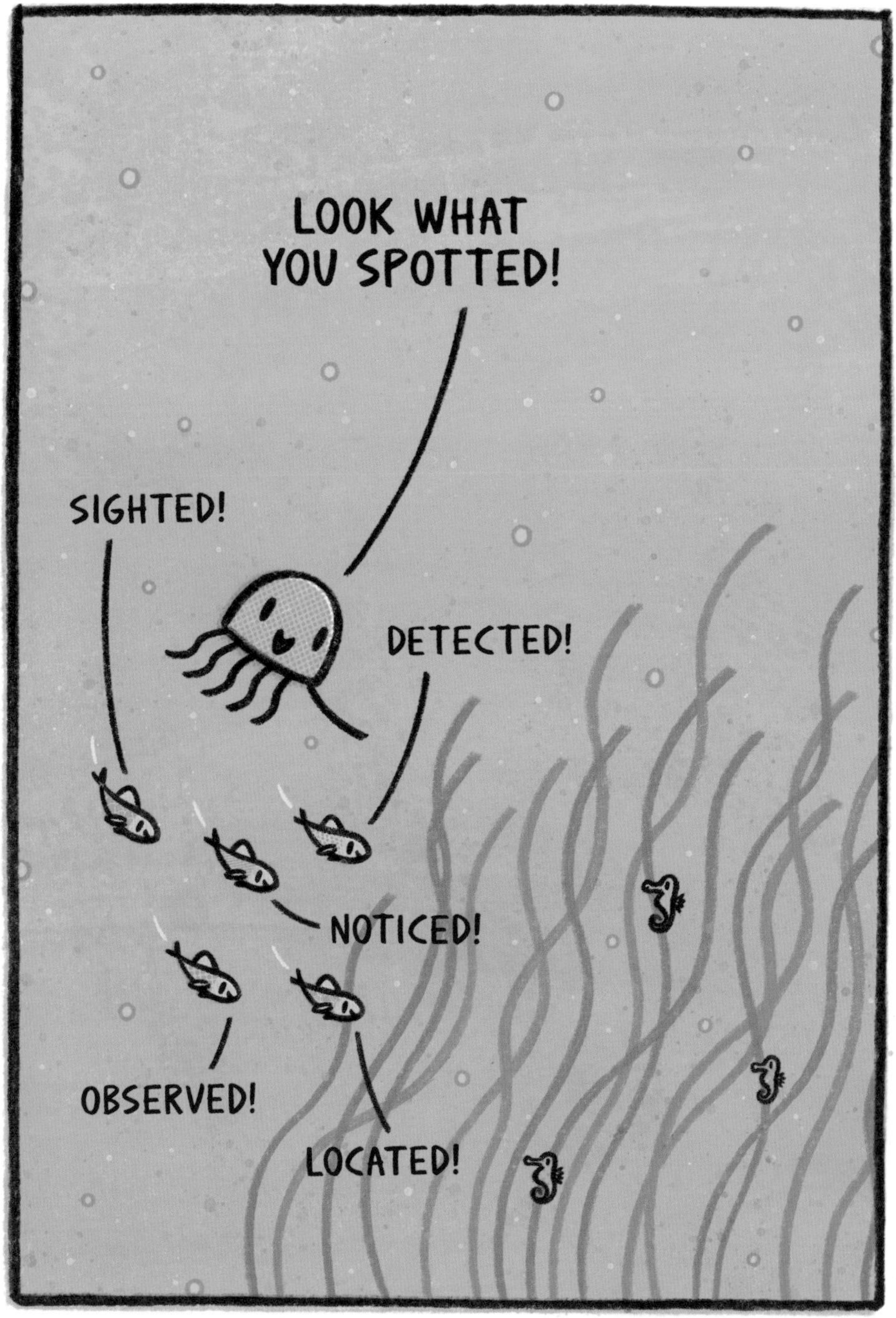
LOOK WHAT YOU SPOTTED!
SIGHTED!
DETECTED!
NOTICED!
OBSERVED!
LOCATED!

EXACTLY THIRTY-THREE MINUTES LATER . . .

THE RESULTS!

TEAM JELLY

A.K.A. SCIENCE SQUAD

1. SEAHORSES ARE FISH!

2. MALE SEAHORSES CAN GIVE BIRTH TO MORE THAN 1,000 BABIES AT ONCE!

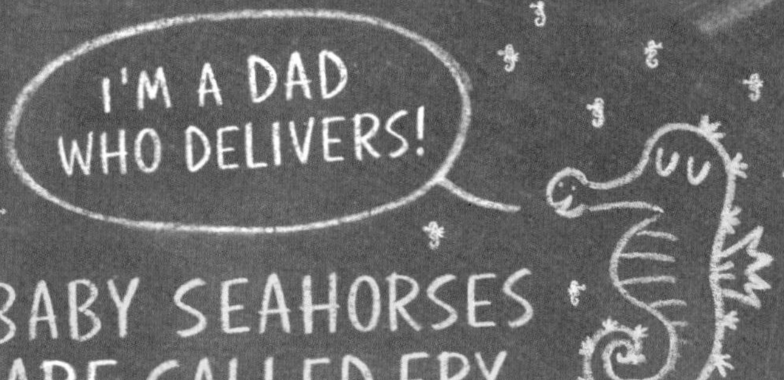
I'M A DAD WHO DELIVERS!

3. BABY SEAHORSES ARE CALLED FRY.

4. SEAHORSES CAN CHANGE COLOR!

TEAM NARWHAL
A.K.A. FUN FINDERS

① THERE ARE 22 SPECIES OF ALBATROSS.

② THE WINGSPAN OF THE WANDERING ALBATROSS CAN REACH UP TO 12 FEET— OVER 3.5 METERS!

③ THEY CAN FLY AS MUCH AS 10,000 MILES (ABOUT 16,000 KM) IN ONE GO.

I'VE GOT A LOT OF SKY MILES!

④ THEY CAN LIVE 50+ YEARS!

⑤ THEY CAN FLY OVER 50mph (ABOUT 80km/h)!

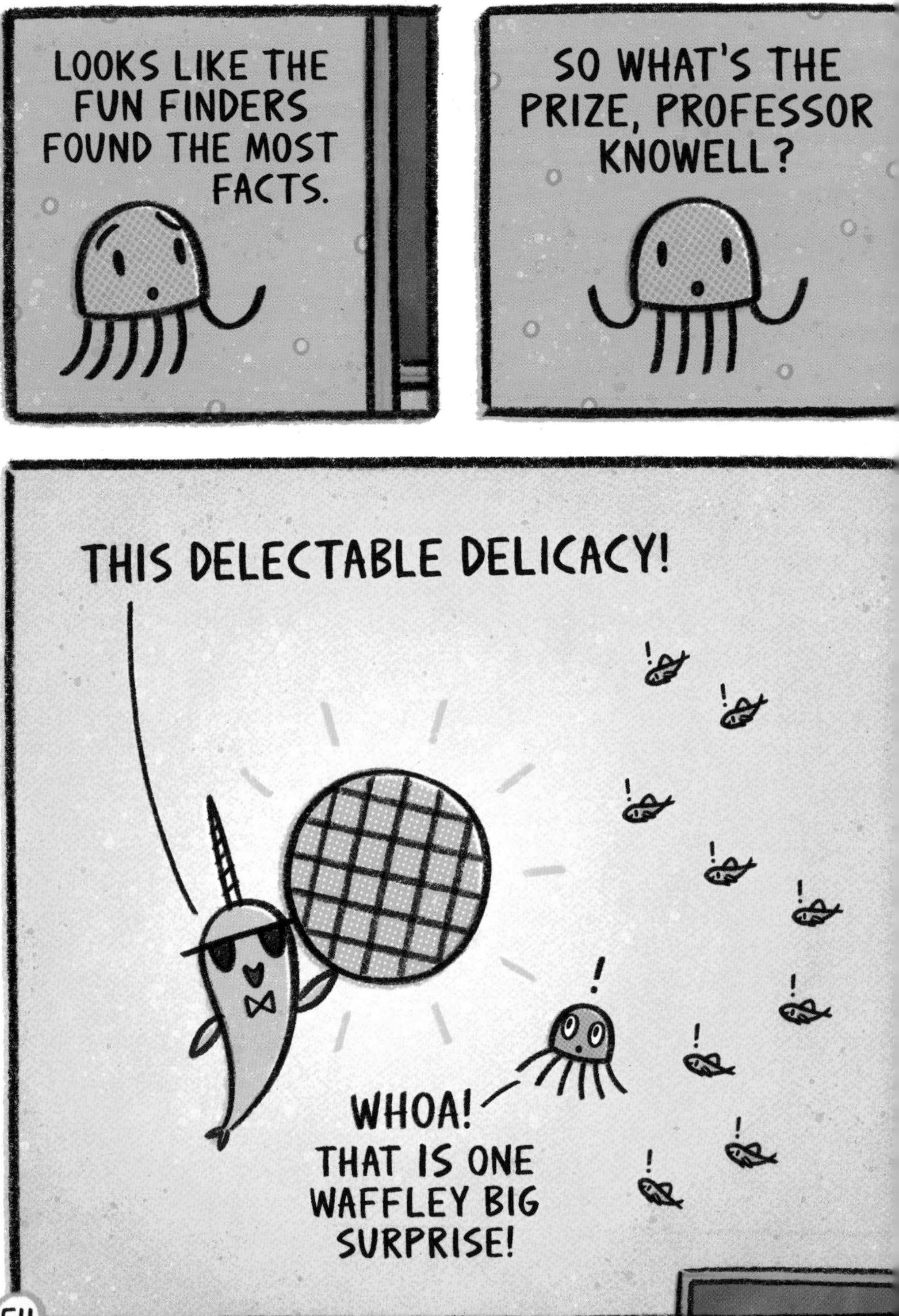
LOOKS LIKE THE FUN FINDERS FOUND THE MOST FACTS.
SO WHAT'S THE PRIZE, PROFESSOR KNOWELL?
THIS DELECTABLE DELICACY!
WHOA! THAT IS ONE WAFFLEY BIG SURPRISE!
!
!
!
!
!
!
!
!
!
!
!

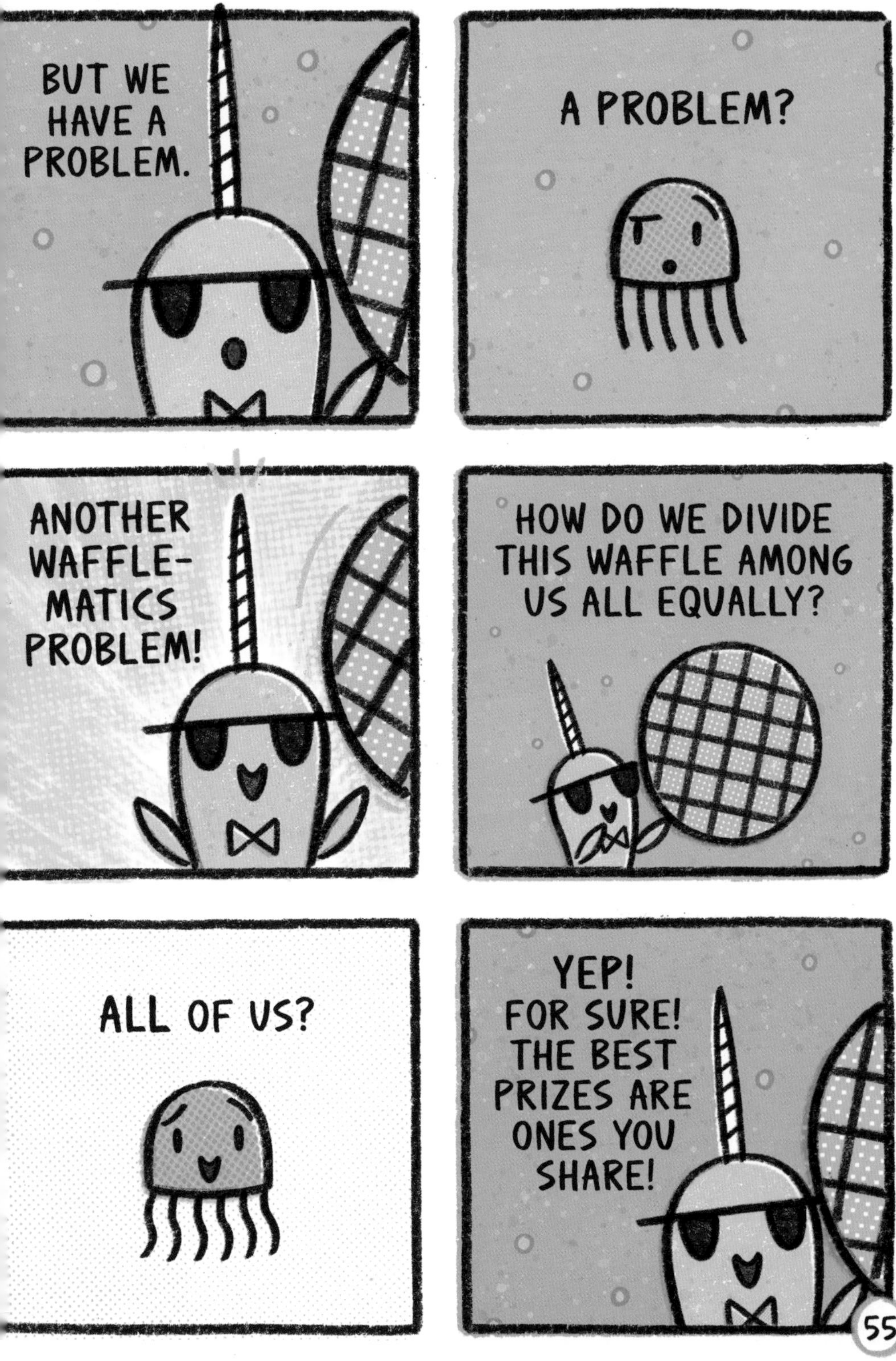
BUT WE HAVE A PROBLEM.
A PROBLEM?
ANOTHER WAFFLE-MATICS PROBLEM!
HOW DO WE DIVIDE THIS WAFFLE AMONG US ALL EQUALLY?
ALL OF US?
YEP! FOR SURE! THE BEST PRIZES ARE ONES YOU SHARE!

BESIDES, MY BELLY IS ALREADY
BURSTING FROM ALL THOSE
WAFFLES I ATE EARLIER!

hee! hee!

TAG! YOU'RE ~~IT!~~

AWESOME!

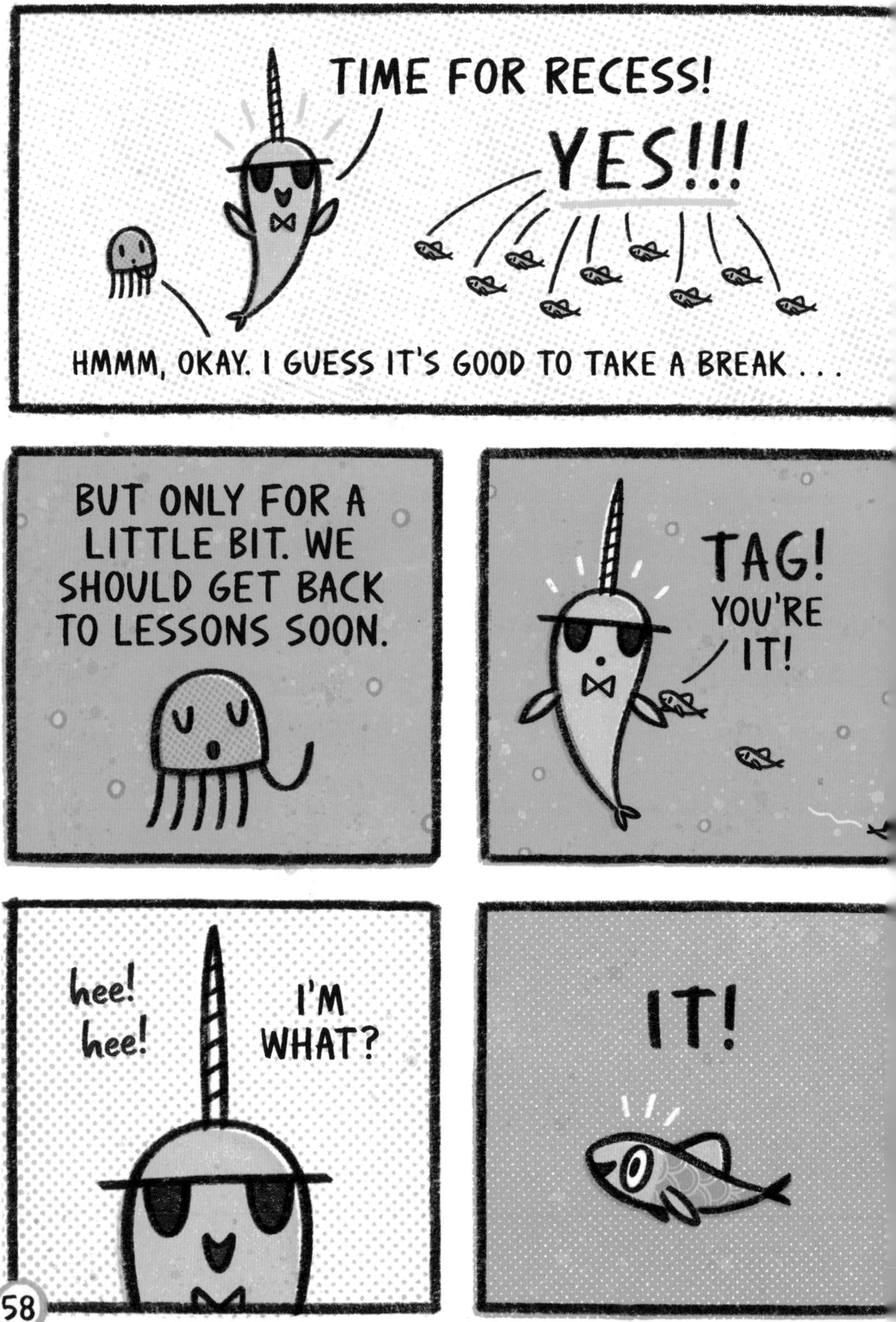
TIME FOR RECESS!
YES!!!
HMMM, OKAY. I GUESS IT'S GOOD TO TAKE A BREAK . . .
BUT ONLY FOR A LITTLE BIT. WE SHOULD GET BACK TO LESSONS SOON.
TAG! YOU'RE IT!
hee! hee!
I'M WHAT?
IT!

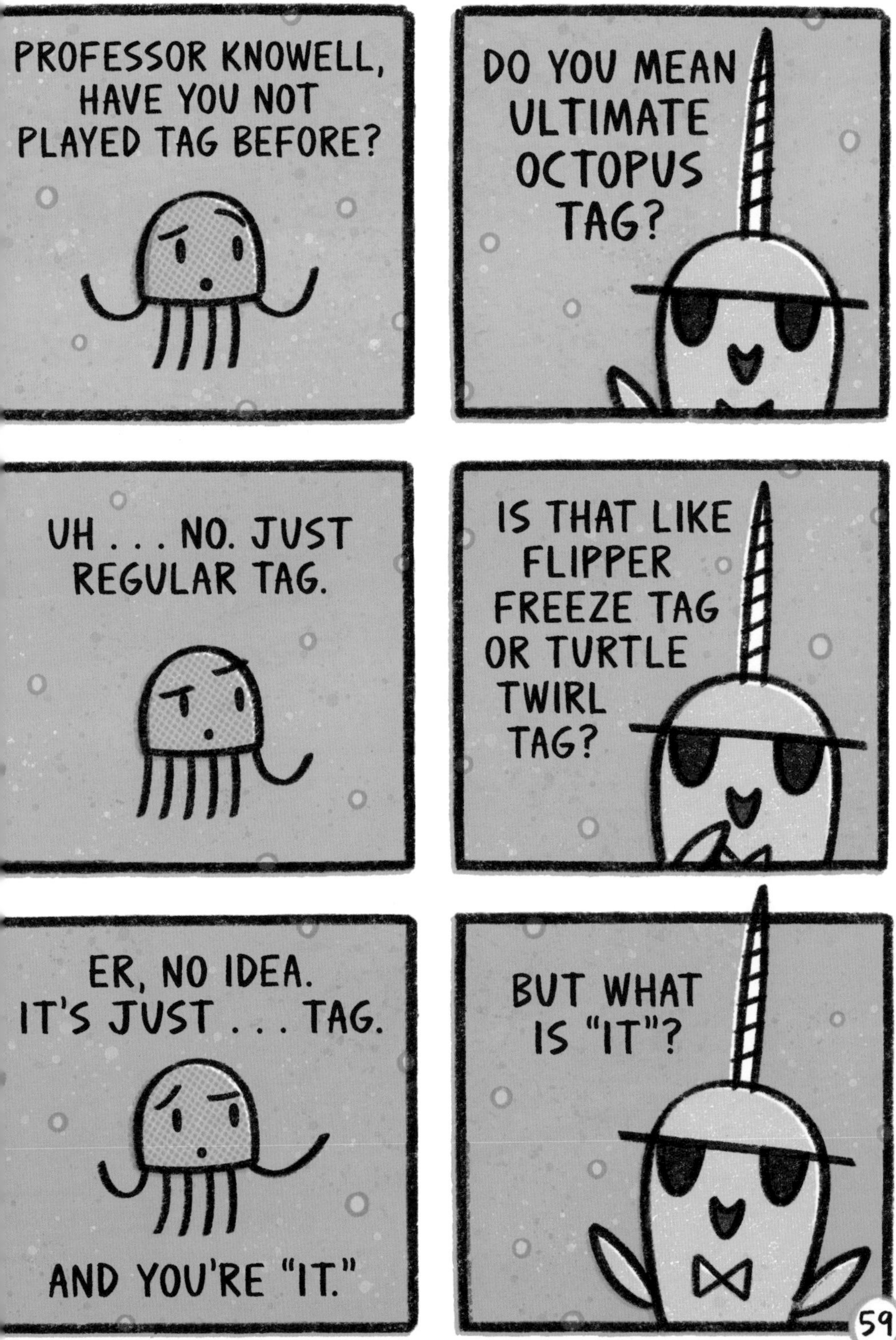
PROFESSOR KNOWELL, HAVE YOU NOT PLAYED TAG BEFORE?
DO YOU MEAN ULTIMATE OCTOPUS TAG?
UH . . . NO. JUST REGULAR TAG.
IS THAT LIKE FLIPPER FREEZE TAG OR TURTLE TWIRL TAG?
ER, NO IDEA. IT'S JUST . . . TAG.
AND YOU'RE "IT."
BUT WHAT IS "IT"?

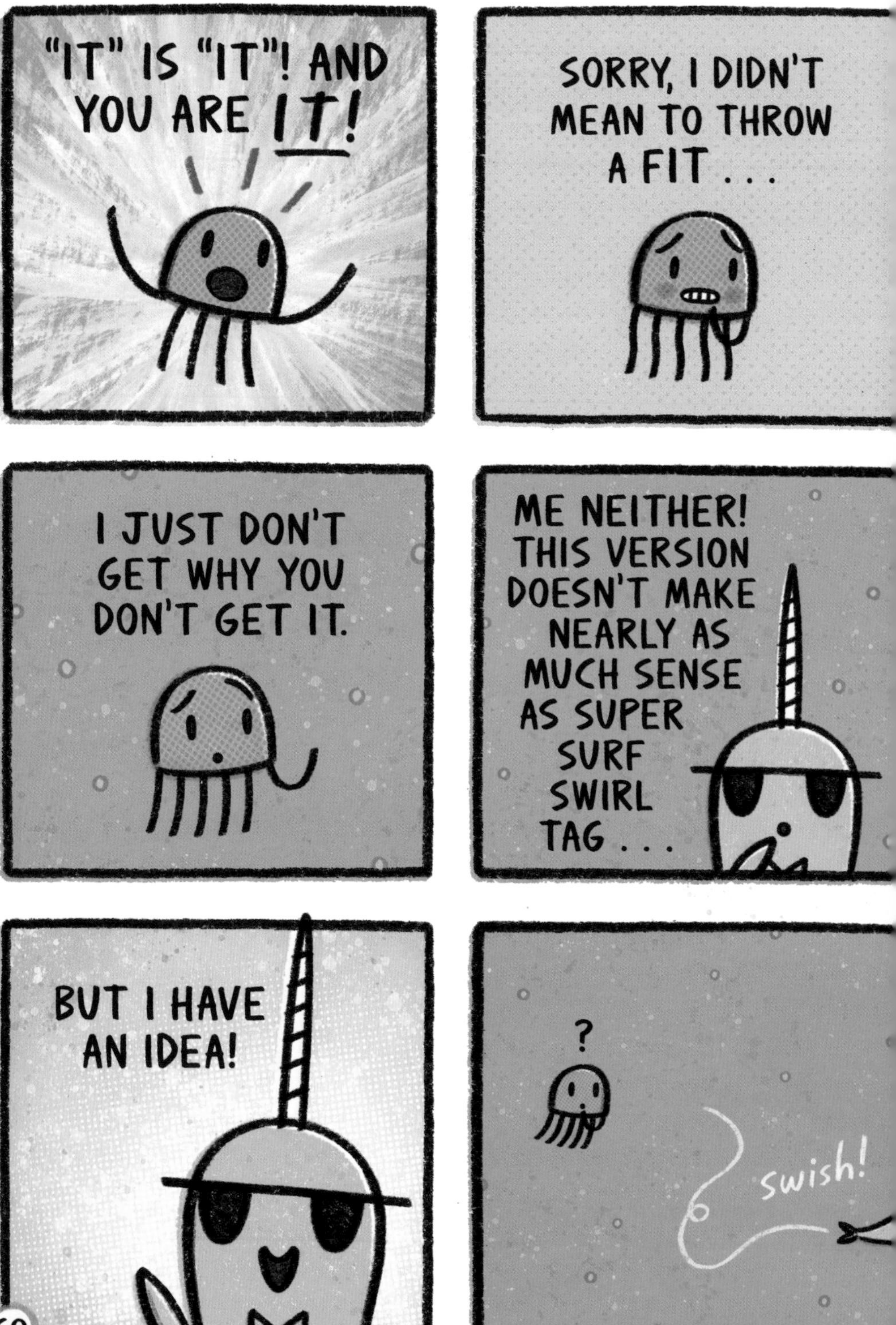
"IT" IS "IT"! AND YOU ARE IT!
SORRY, I DIDN'T MEAN TO THROW A FIT . . .
I JUST DON'T GET WHY YOU DON'T GET IT.
ME NEITHER! THIS VERSION DOESN'T MAKE NEARLY AS MUCH SENSE AS SUPER SURF SWIRL TAG . . .
BUT I HAVE AN IDEA!
?
swish!

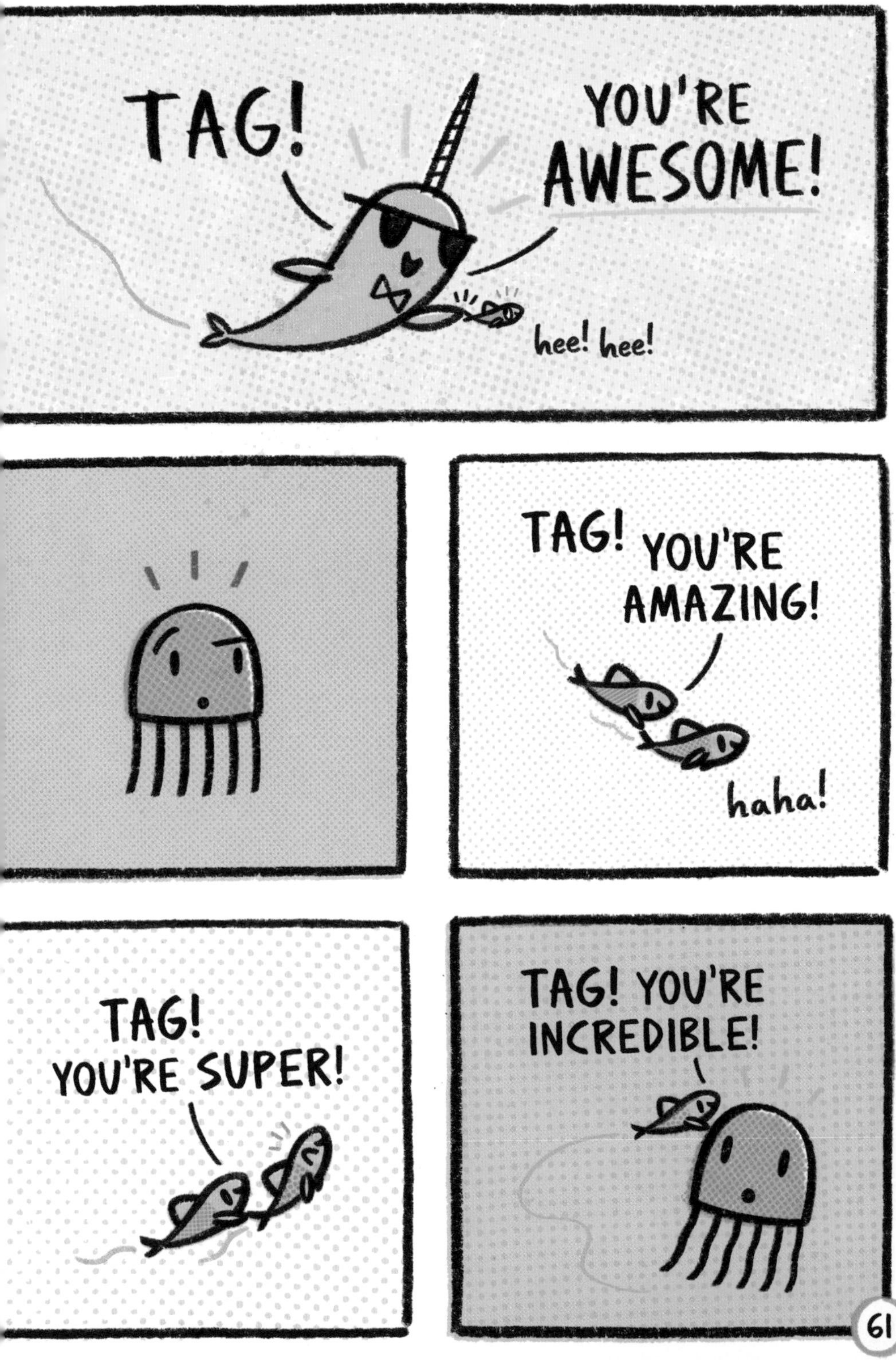
TAG!
YOU'RE AWESOME!
hee! hee!
TAG! YOU'RE AMAZING!
haha!
TAG! YOU'RE SUPER!
TAG! YOU'RE INCREDIBLE!

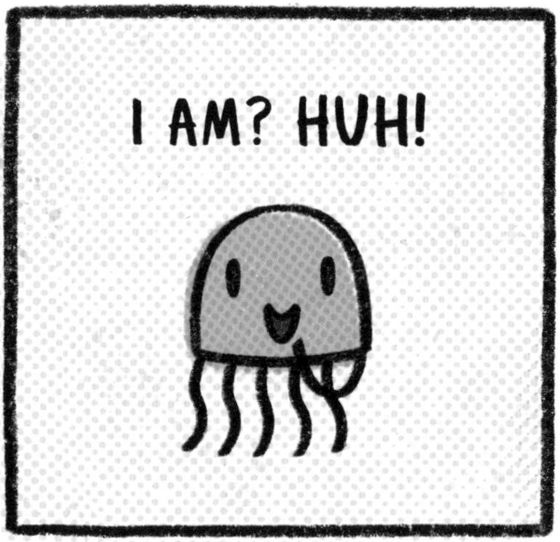
I AM? HUH!

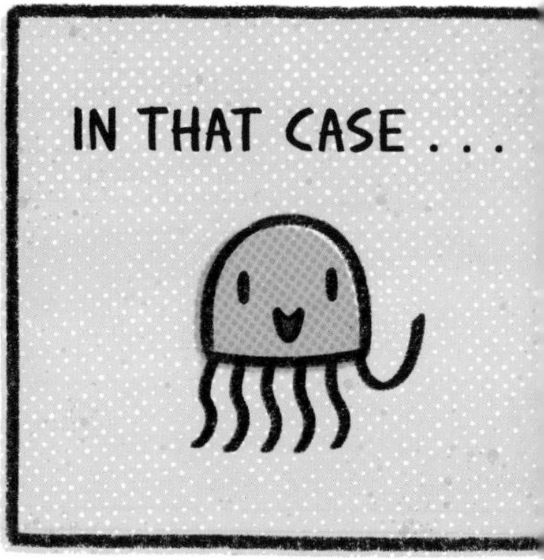
IN THAT CASE . . .

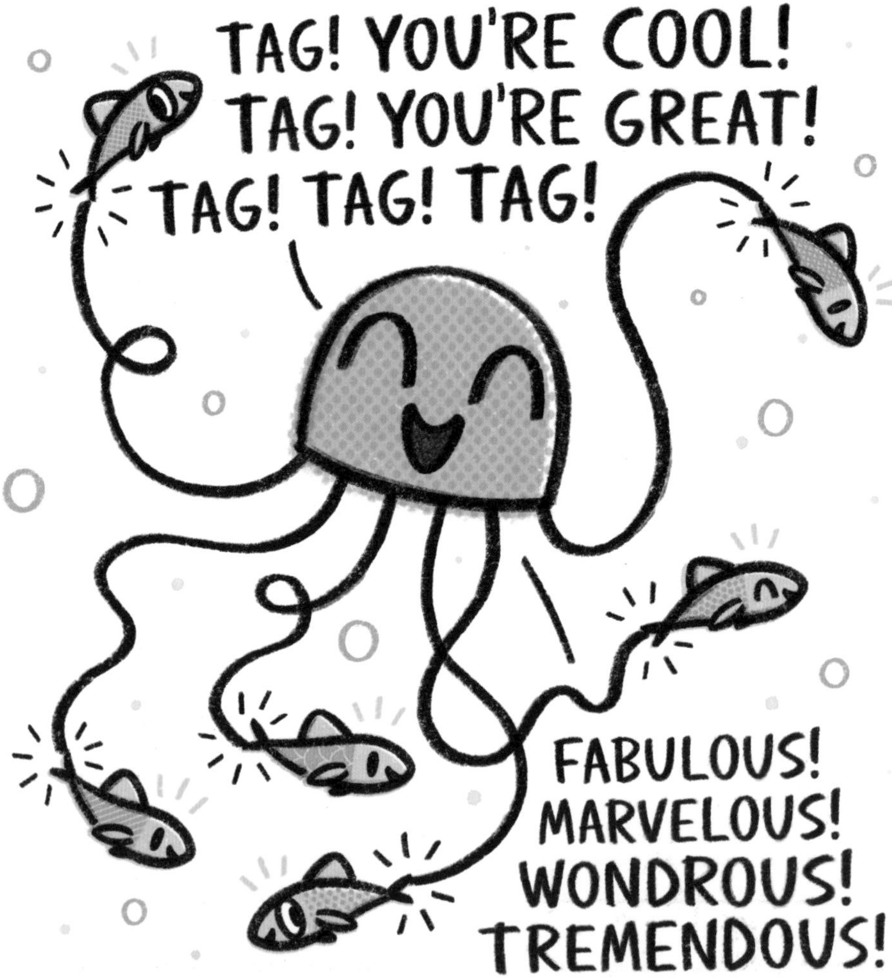
TAG! YOU'RE COOL!
TAG! YOU'RE GREAT!
TAG! TAG! TAG!
FABULOUS!
MARVELOUS!
WONDROUS!
TREMENDOUS!

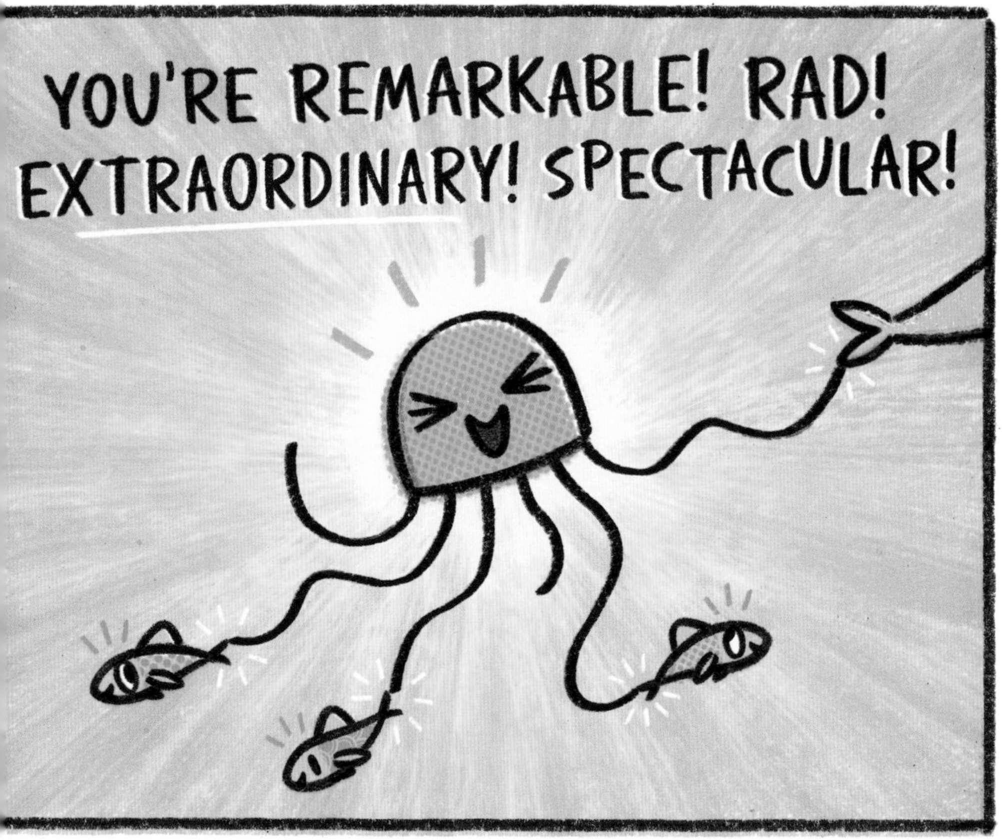
YOU'RE REMARKABLE! RAD! EXTRAORDINARY! SPECTACULAR!

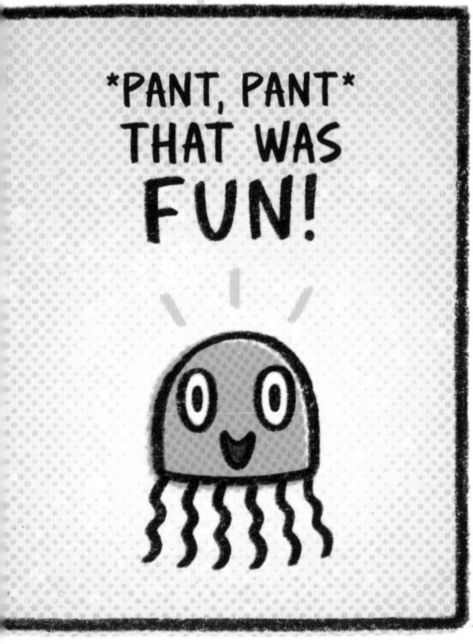
PANT, PANT
THAT WAS FUN!

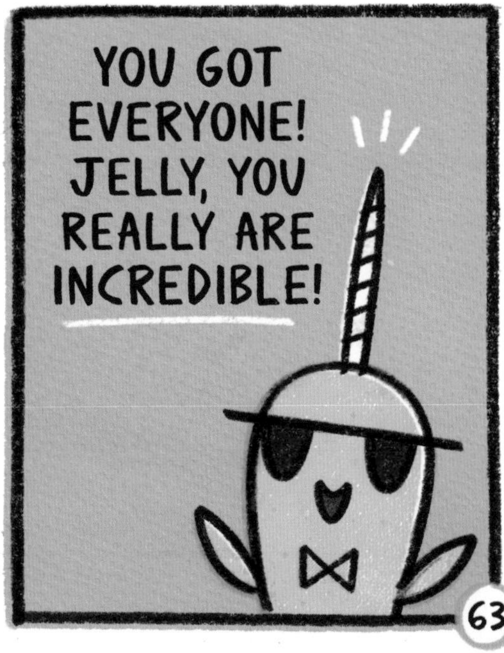
YOU GOT EVERYONE! JELLY, YOU REALLY ARE INCREDIBLE!

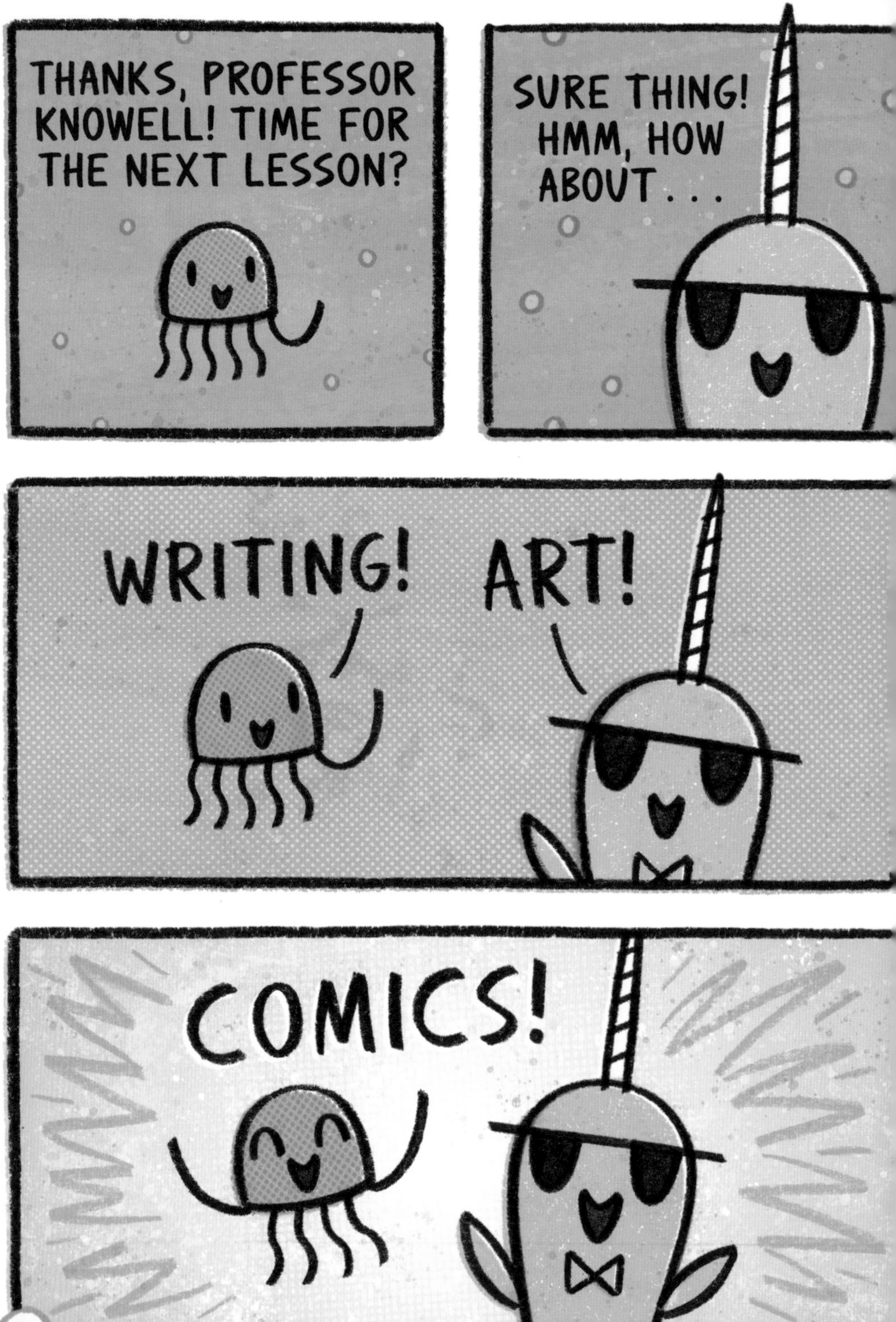
THANKS, PROFESSOR KNOWELL! TIME FOR THE NEXT LESSON?
SURE THING! HMM, HOW ABOUT . . .
WRITING!
ART!
COMICS!

SUPER WAFFLE
AND <u>STRAWBERRY</u> SIDEKICK

VS.

The Mucus Monster

by

Professor Knowell, Jelly, Fin, Finneas,
Finnie, Finbar, Finley, Finnegan,
Delfina, Finch and Finnard

ONE DAY WHEN SUPER WAFFLE AND
STRAWBERRY SIDEKICK WERE HAVING A
BUBBLE BLOWING BATTLE . . .

EEK!

ICK!

ACK!

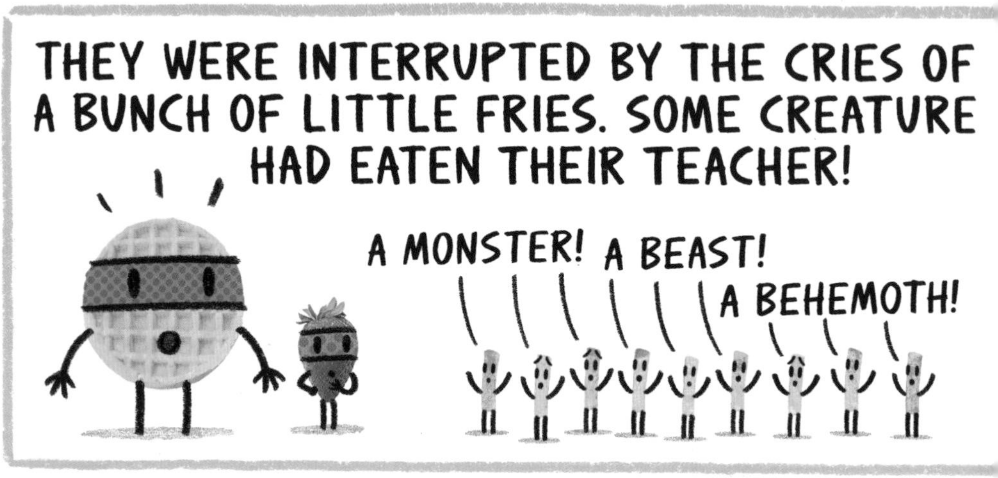
THEY WERE INTERRUPTED BY THE CRIES OF A BUNCH OF LITTLE FRIES. SOME CREATURE HAD EATEN THEIR TEACHER!
A MONSTER!
A BEAST!
A BEHEMOTH!

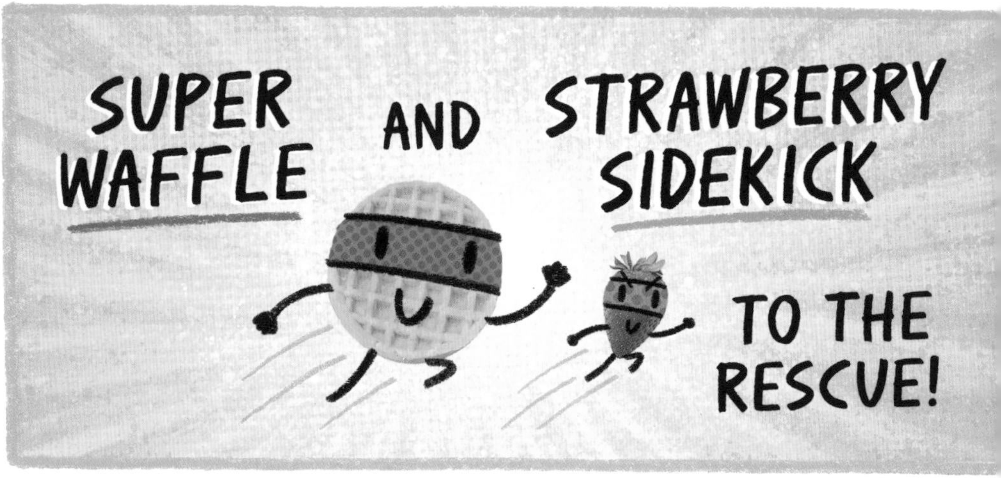
SUPER WAFFLE
AND
STRAWBERRY SIDEKICK
TO THE RESCUE!

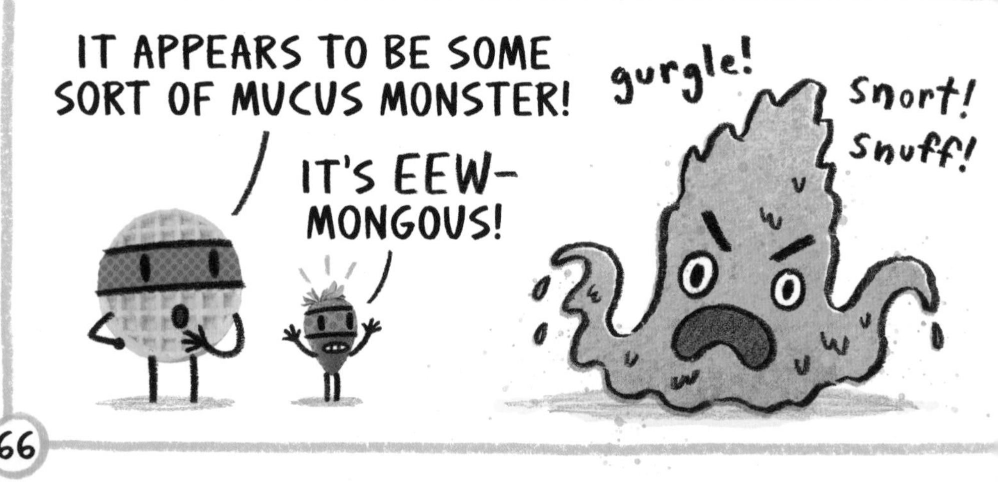
IT APPEARS TO BE SOME SORT OF MUCUS MONSTER!
IT'S EEW-MONGOUS!
gurgle!
Snort!
Snuff!

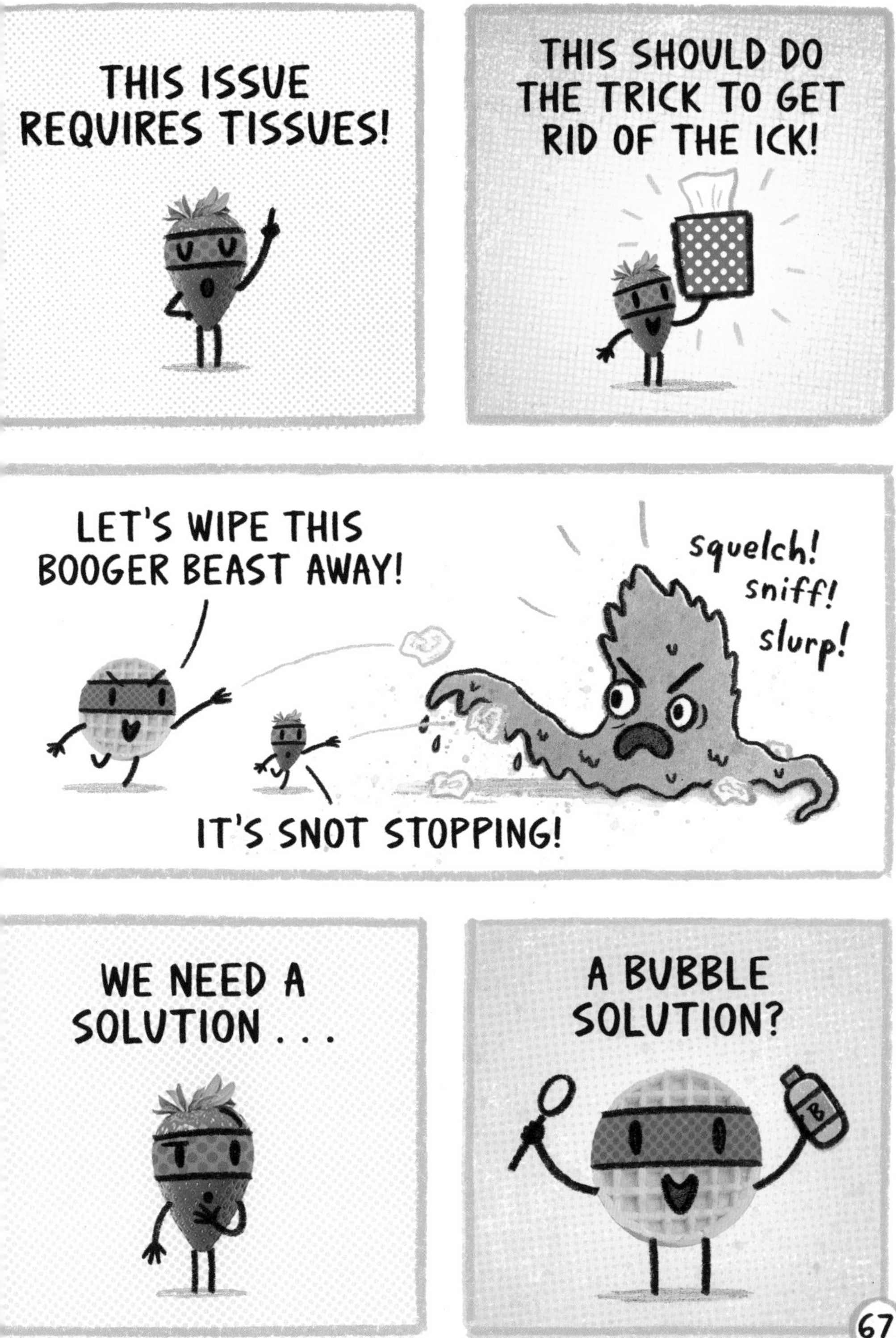

THIS ISSUE REQUIRES TISSUES!
THIS SHOULD DO THE TRICK TO GET RID OF THE ICK!
LET'S WIPE THIS BOOGER BEAST AWAY!
squelch!
sniff!
slurp!
IT'S SNOT STOPPING!
WE NEED A SOLUTION . . .
A BUBBLE SOLUTION?
B

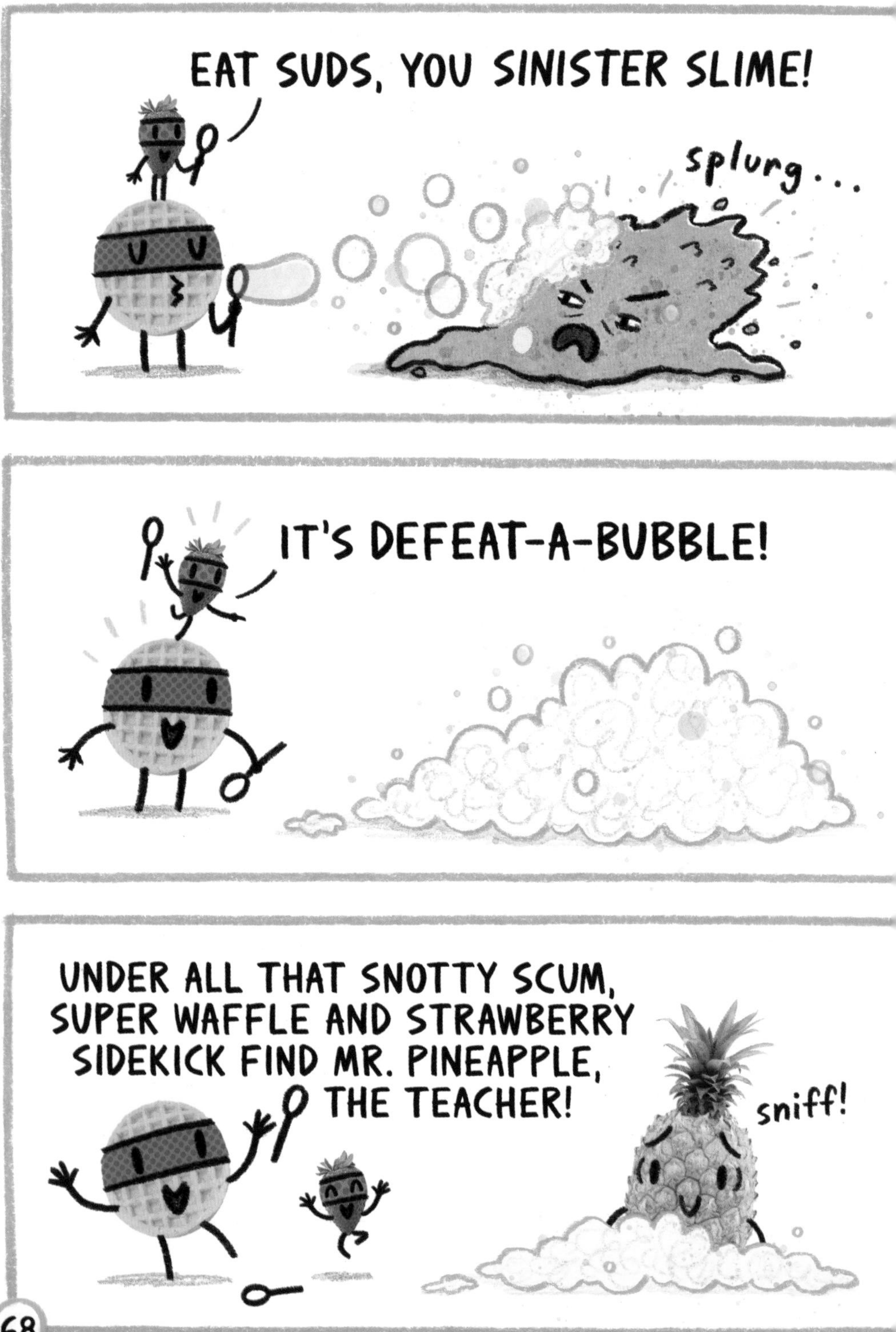
EAT SUDS, YOU SINISTER SLIME!
splurg...
IT'S DEFEAT-A-BUBBLE!
UNDER ALL THAT SNOTTY SCUM, SUPER WAFFLE AND STRAWBERRY SIDEKICK FIND MR. PINEAPPLE, THE TEACHER!
sniff!

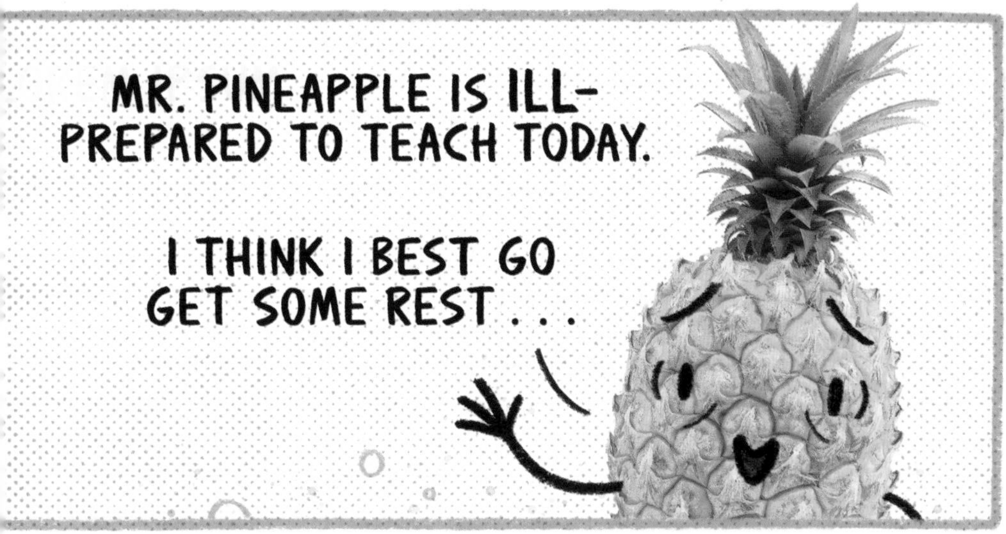
MR. PINEAPPLE IS ILL-PREPARED TO TEACH TODAY.
I THINK I BEST GO GET SOME REST . . .

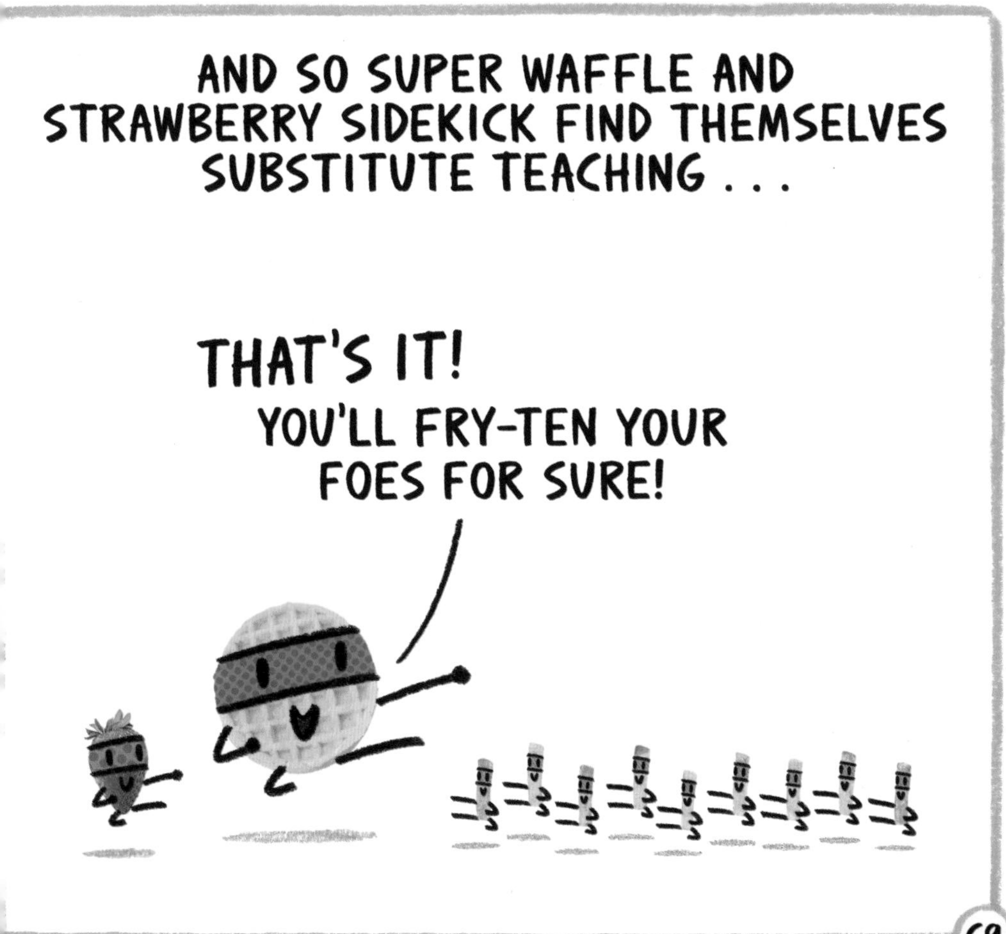
AND SO SUPER WAFFLE AND STRAWBERRY SIDEKICK FIND THEMSELVES SUBSTITUTE TEACHING . . .
THAT'S IT!
YOU'LL FRY-TEN YOUR FOES FOR SURE!

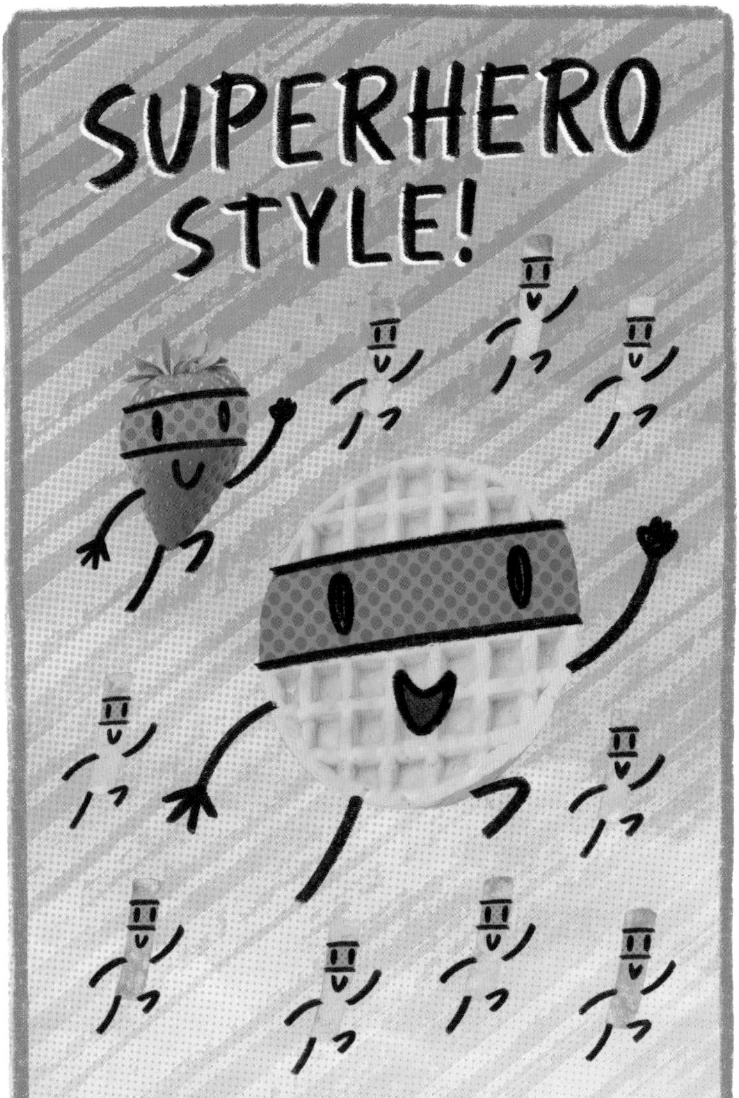
SUPERHERO
STYLE!

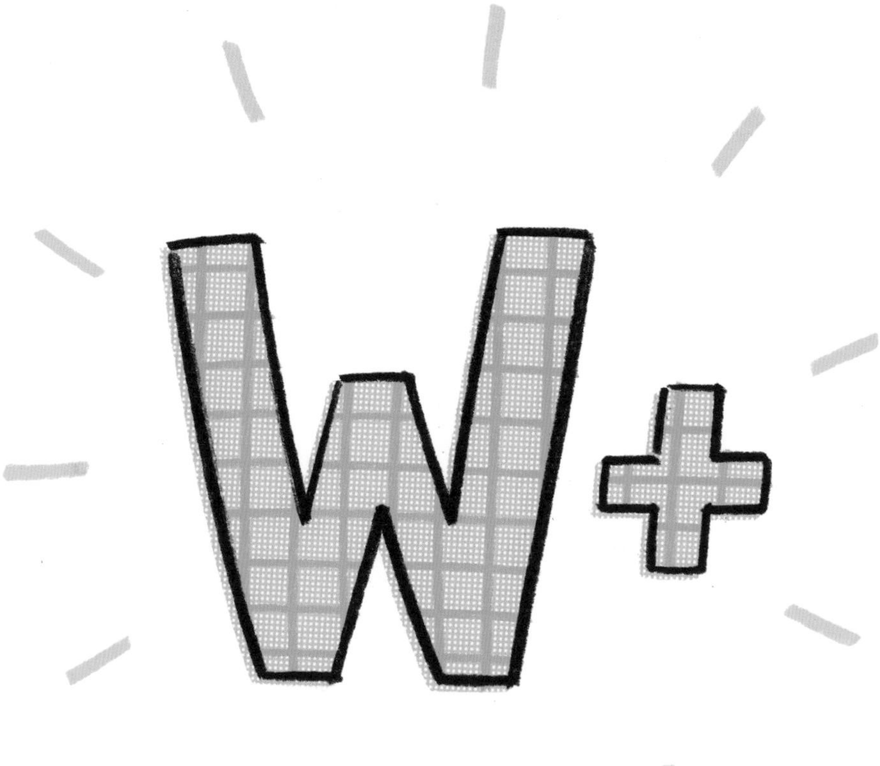
W+

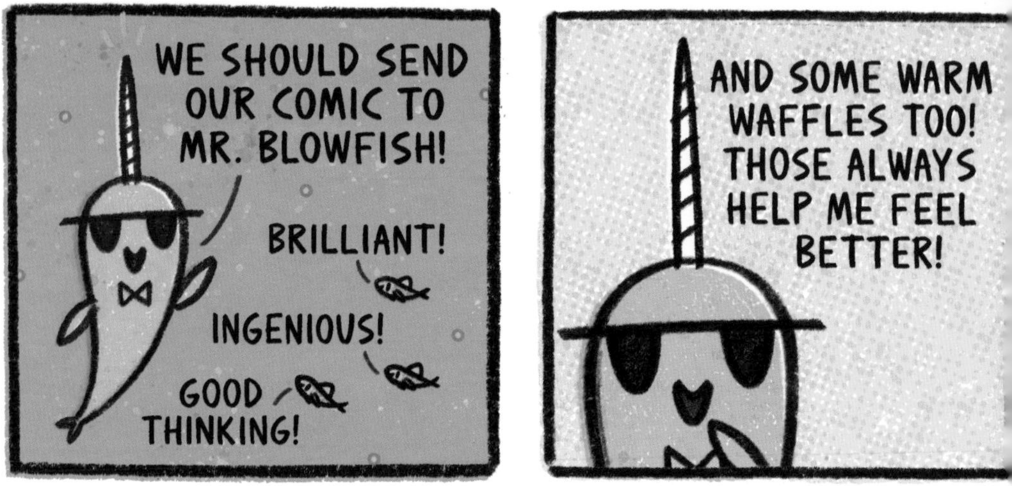
WE SHOULD SEND OUR COMIC TO MR. BLOWFISH!
BRILLIANT!
INGENIOUS!
GOOD THINKING!
AND SOME WARM WAFFLES TOO! THOSE ALWAYS HELP ME FEEL BETTER!

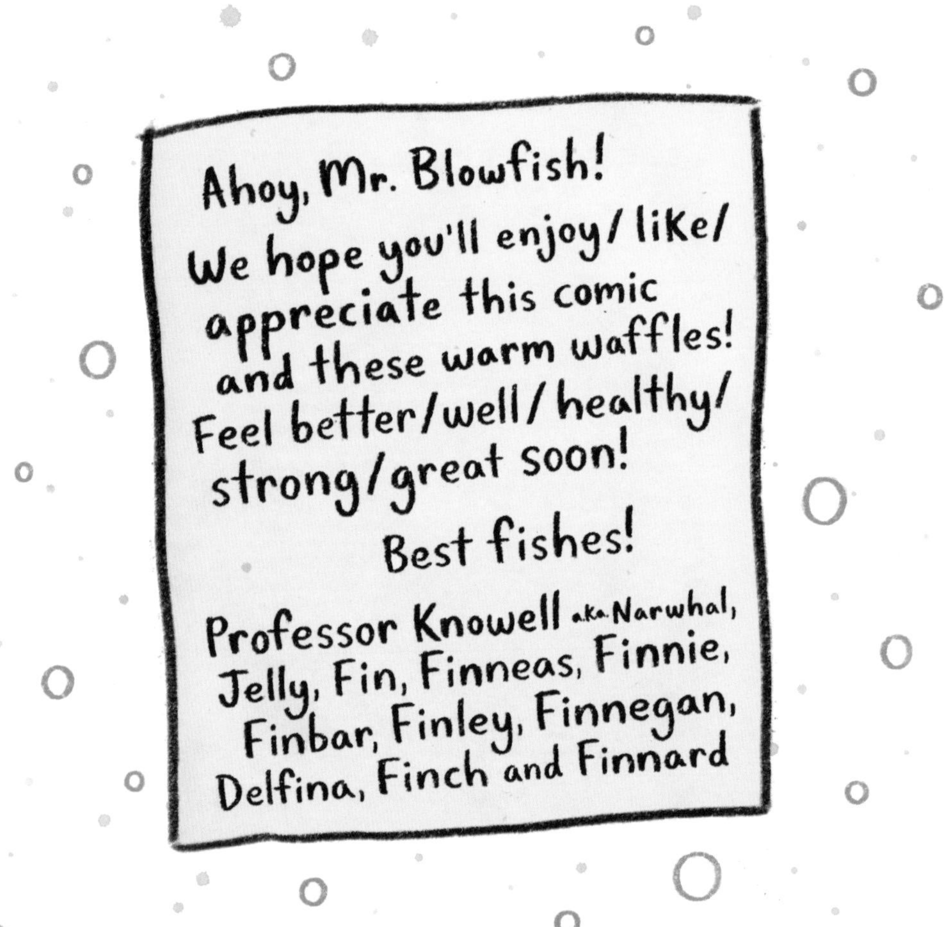
Ahoy, Mr. Blowfish!
We hope you'll enjoy/like/appreciate this comic and these warm waffles!
Feel better/well/healthy/strong/great soon!
Best fishes!
Professor Knowell a.k.a. Narwhal, Jelly, Fin, Finneas, Finnie, Finbar, Finley, Finnegan, Delfina, Finch and Finnard

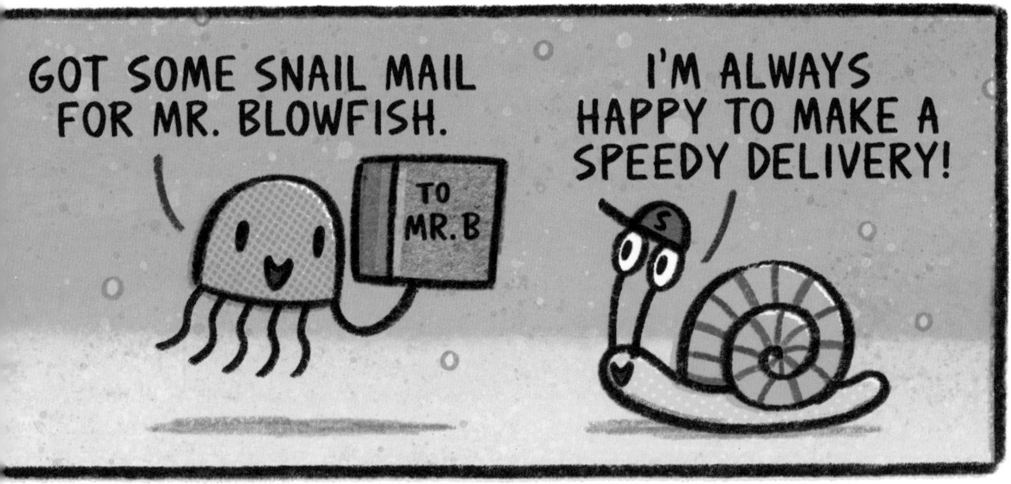
GOT SOME SNAIL MAIL FOR MR. BLOWFISH.
TO MR. B
I'M ALWAYS HAPPY TO MAKE A SPEEDY DELIVERY!

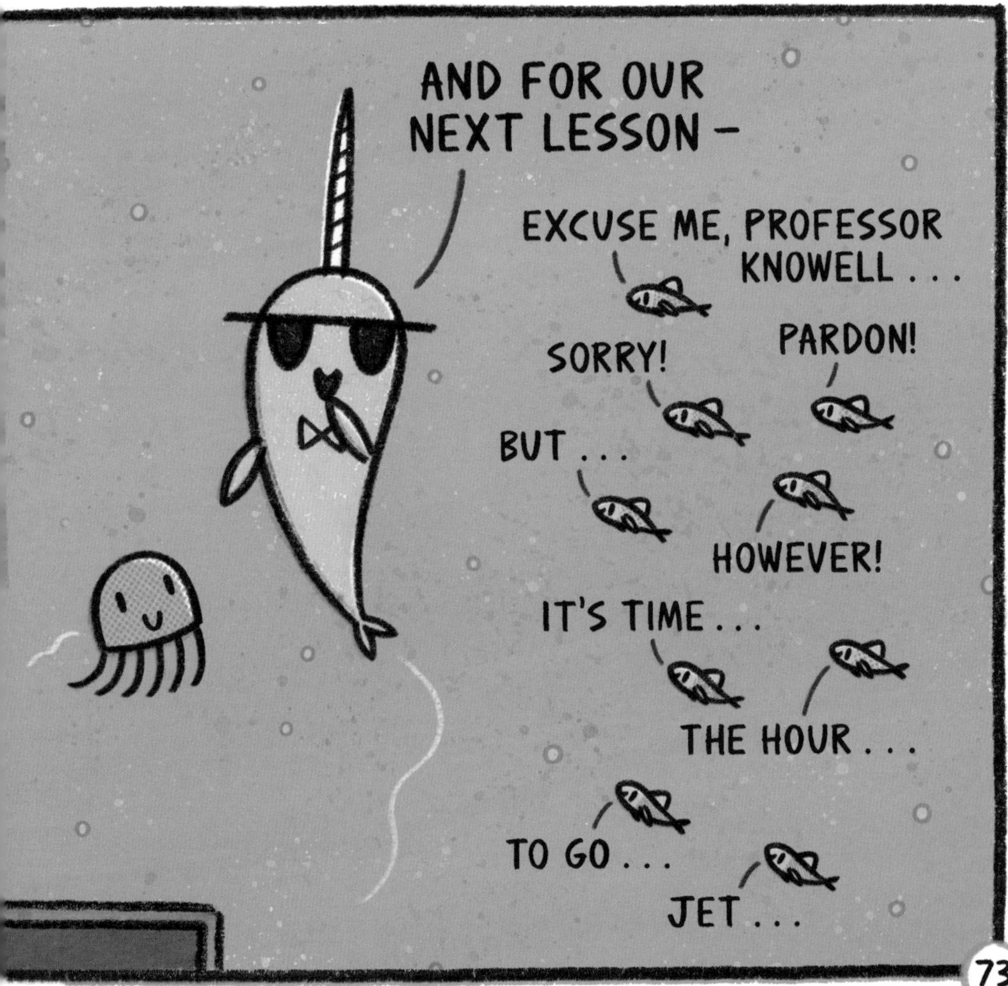
AND FOR OUR NEXT LESSON –
EXCUSE ME, PROFESSOR KNOWELL . . .
SORRY!
PARDON!
BUT . . .
HOWEVER!
IT'S TIME . . .
THE HOUR . . .
TO GO . . .
JET . . .

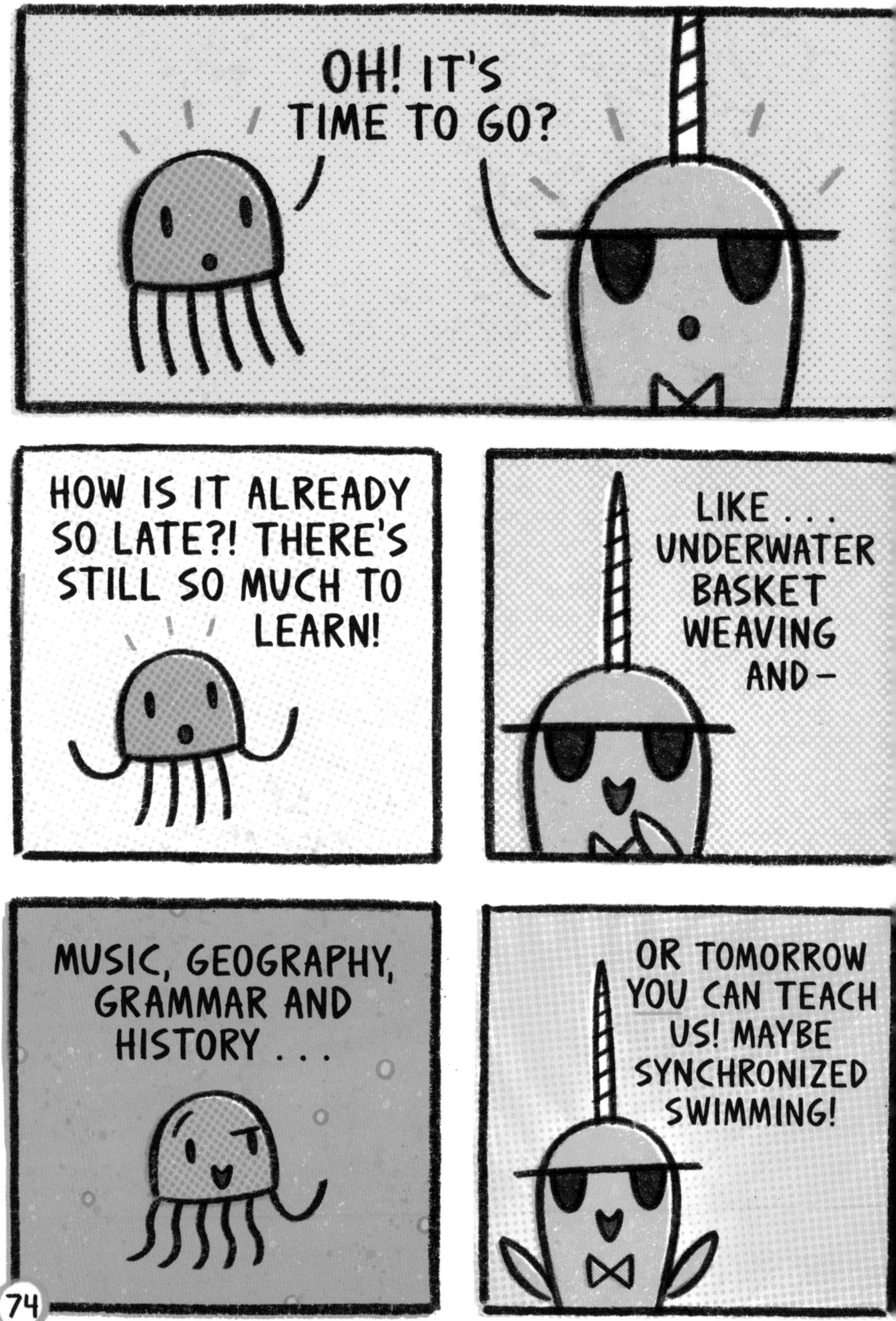
OH! IT'S TIME TO GO?
HOW IS IT ALREADY SO LATE?! THERE'S STILL SO MUCH TO LEARN!
LIKE . . . UNDERWATER BASKET WEAVING AND—
MUSIC, GEOGRAPHY, GRAMMAR AND HISTORY . . .
OR TOMORROW YOU CAN TEACH US! MAYBE SYNCHRONIZED SWIMMING!

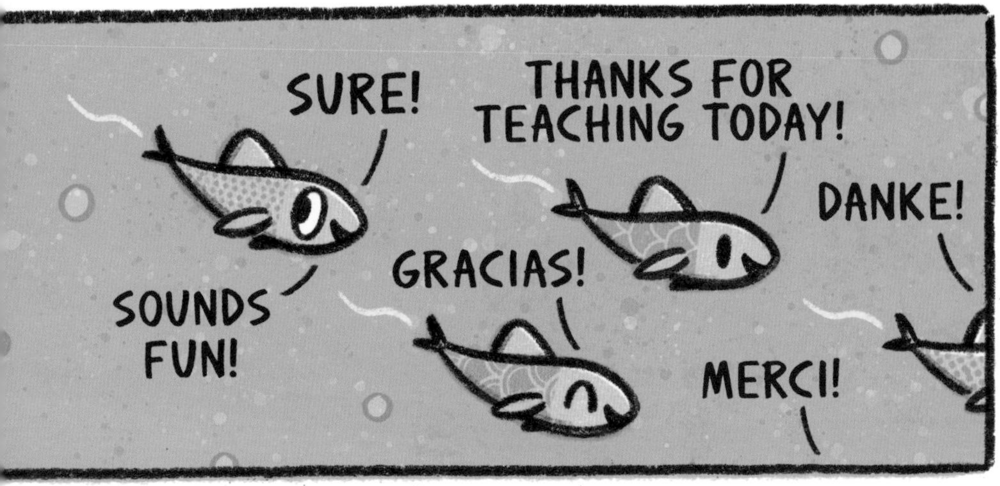
SURE!
THANKS FOR TEACHING TODAY!
DANKE!
SOUNDS FUN!
GRACIAS!
MERCI!

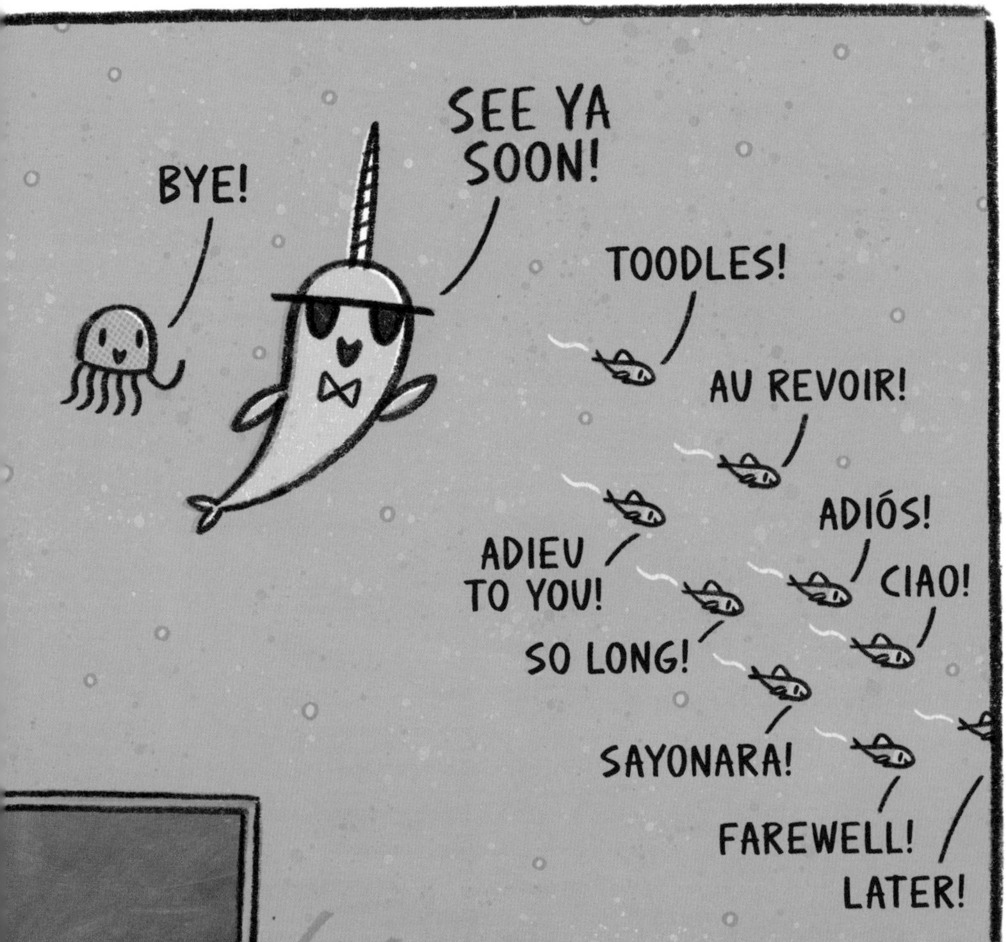
BYE!
SEE YA SOON!
TOODLES!
AU REVOIR!
ADIÓS!
ADIEU TO YOU!
CIAO!
SO LONG!
SAYONARA!
FAREWELL!
LATER!

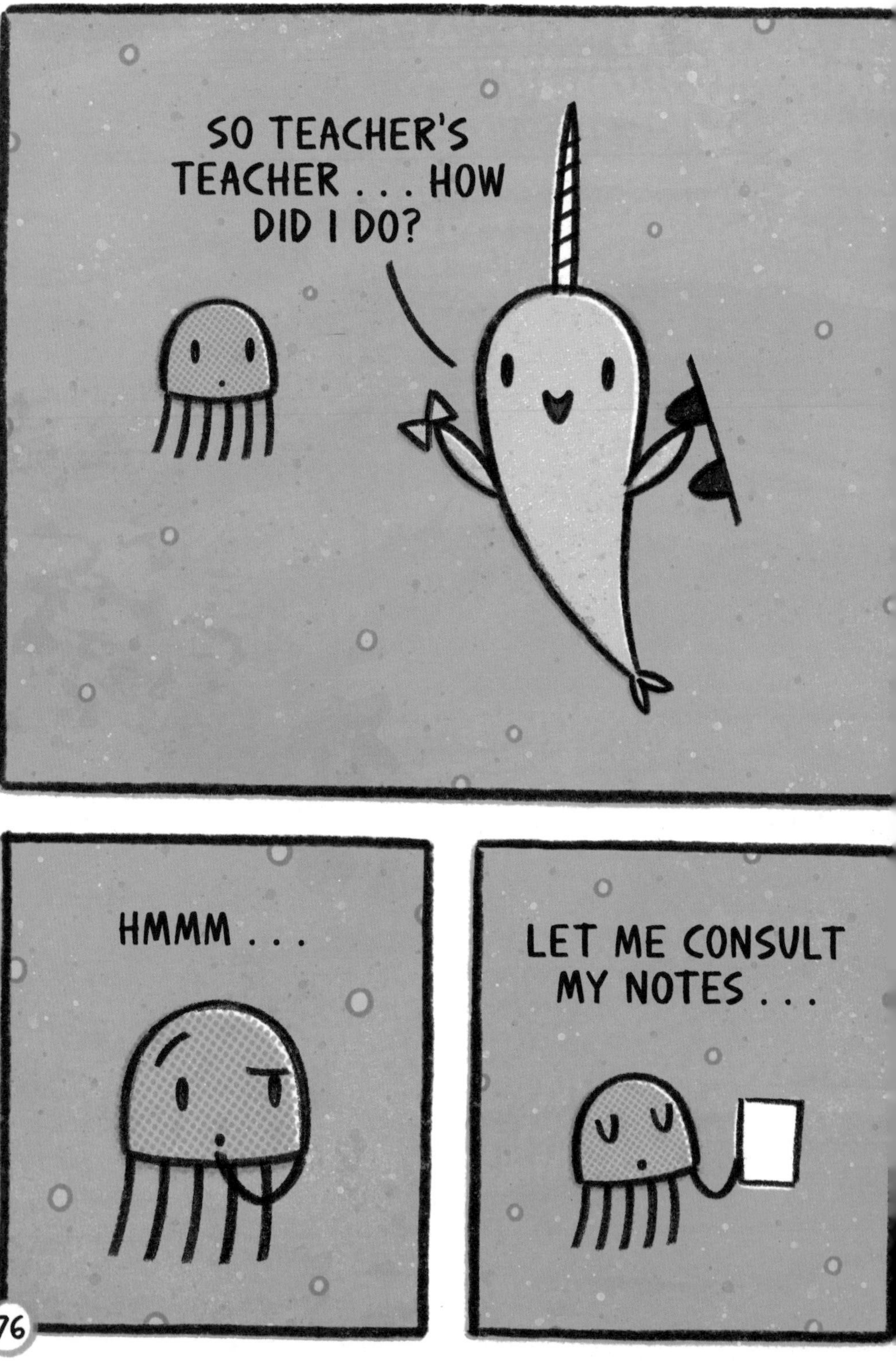
SO TEACHER'S TEACHER . . . HOW DID I DO?
HMMM . . .
LET ME CONSULT MY NOTES . . .

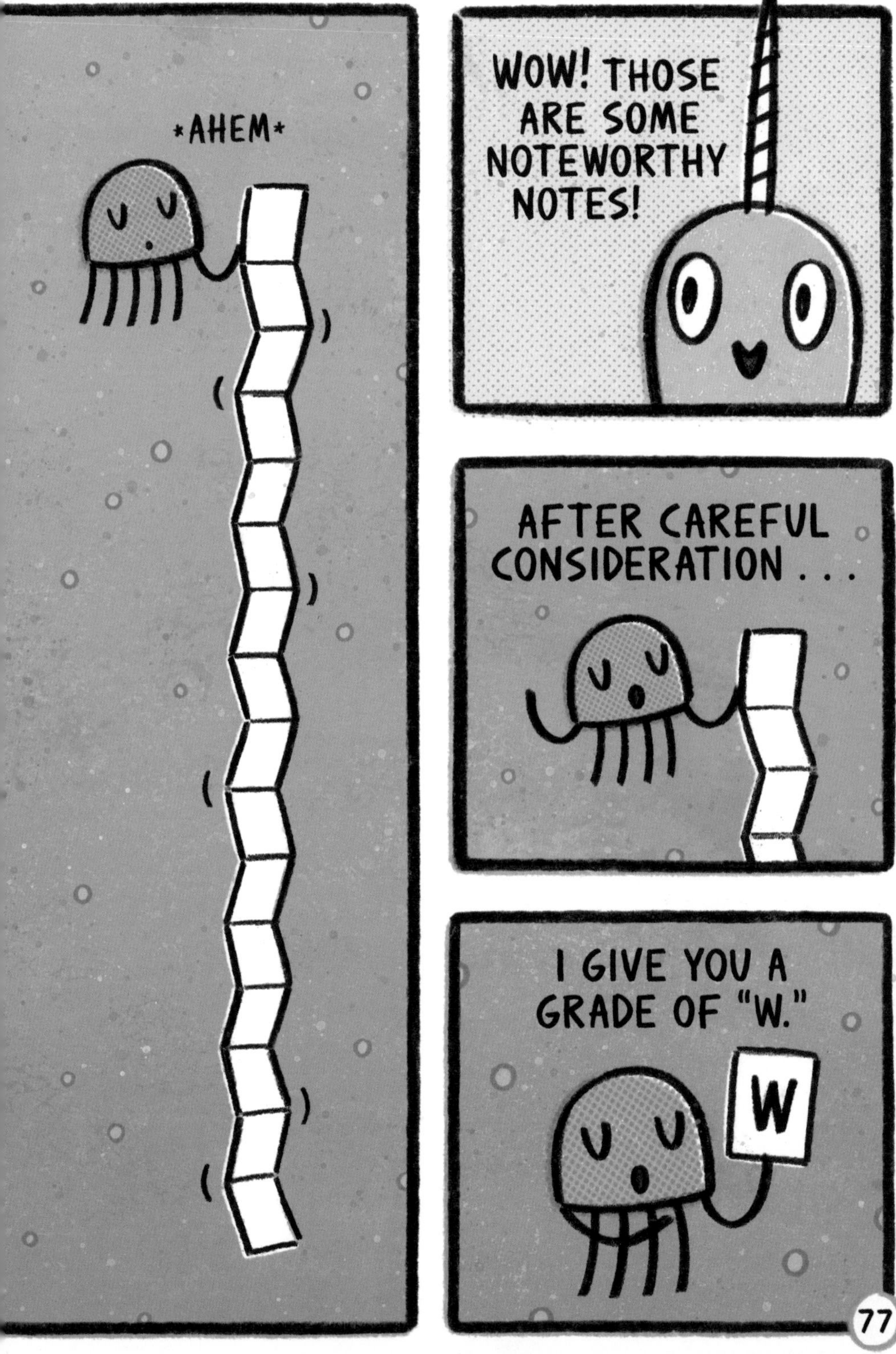
AHEM
WOW! THOSE ARE SOME NOTEWORTHY NOTES!
AFTER CAREFUL CONSIDERATION . . .
I GIVE YOU A GRADE OF "W."
W

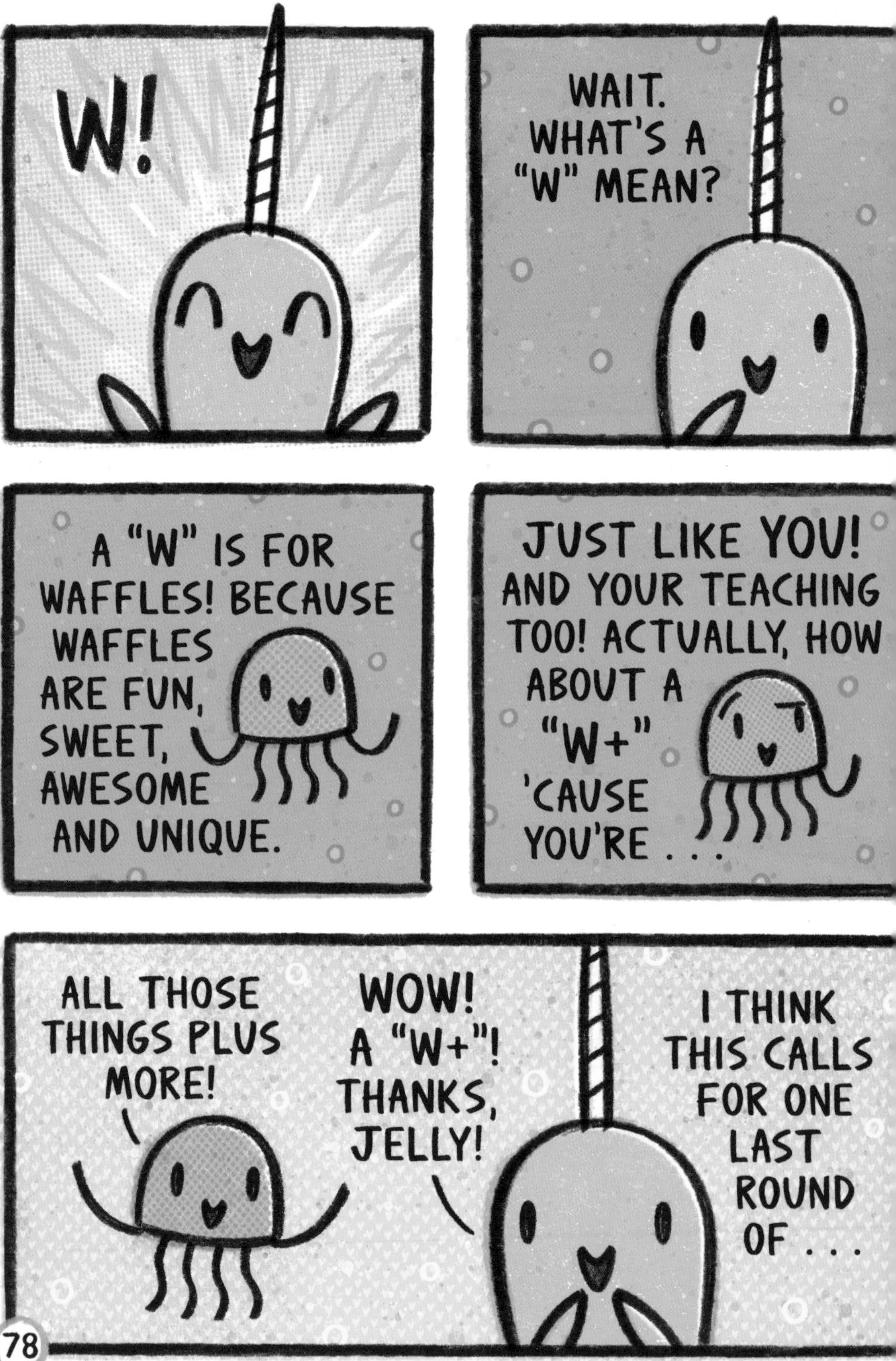
W!
WAIT. WHAT'S A "W" MEAN?
A "W" IS FOR WAFFLES! BECAUSE WAFFLES ARE FUN, SWEET, AWESOME AND UNIQUE.
JUST LIKE YOU! AND YOUR TEACHING TOO! ACTUALLY, HOW ABOUT A "W+" 'CAUSE YOU'RE . . .
ALL THOSE THINGS PLUS MORE!
WOW! A "W+"! THANKS, JELLY!
I THINK THIS CALLS FOR ONE LAST ROUND OF . . .

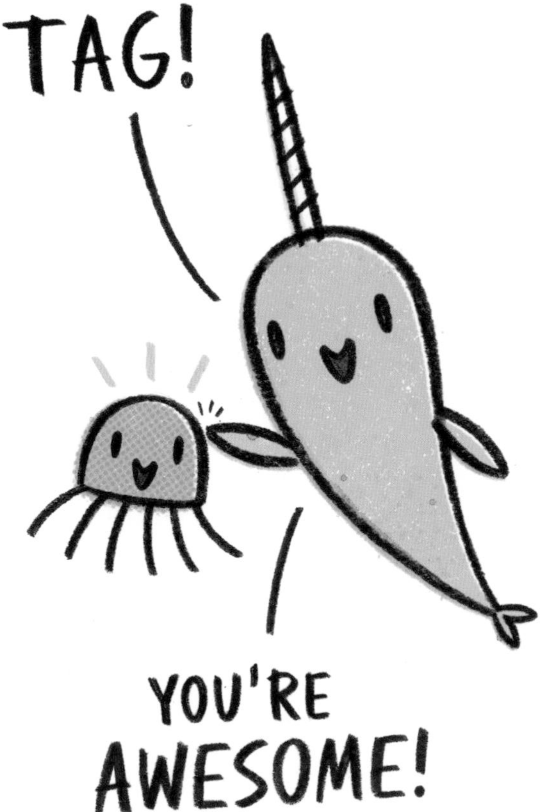
TAG!
YOU'RE
AWESOME!

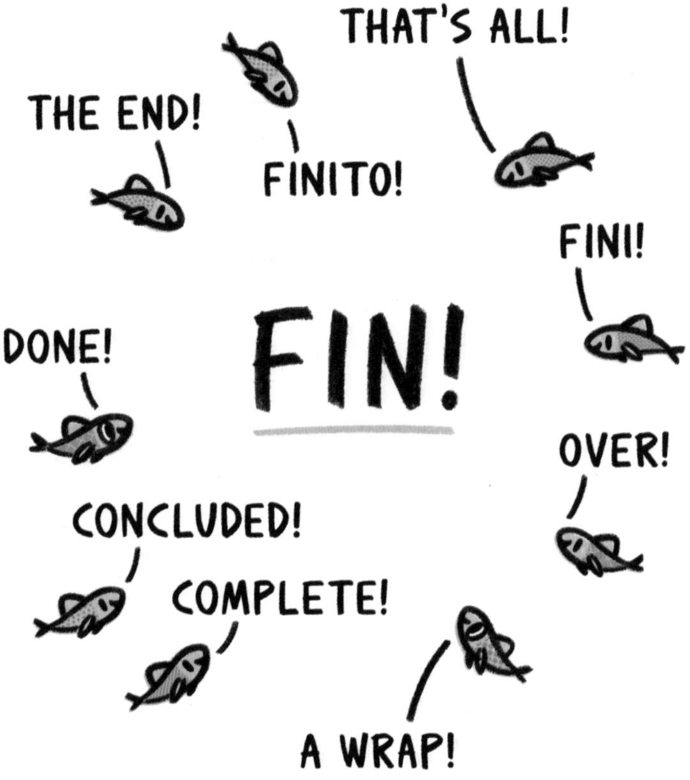
FIN!
THE END!
FINITO!
THAT'S ALL!
FINI!
OVER!
A WRAP!
COMPLETE!
CONCLUDED!
DONE!